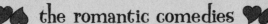 the romantic comedies

# Sea of Love

**JAMIE PONTI**

Simon Pulse

New York London Toronto Sydney

SIMON PULSE
An imprint of Simon & Schuster Children's Publishing Division
1230 Avenue of the Americas, New York, NY 10020
Copyright © 2008 by James Ponti
All rights reserved, including the right of reproduction
in whole or in part in any form.
SIMON PULSE and colophon are registered trademarks
of Simon & Schuster, Inc.
Designed by Ann Zeak
The text of this book was set in Garamond 3.
Manufactured in the United States of America
First Simon Pulse edition December 2008
10 9 8 7 6 5 4 3 2
Library of Congress Control Number 2008927214
ISBN-13: 978-1-4169-6791-0
ISBN-10: 1-4169-6791-5

For my mother

# Acknowledgments

Writing can be a lonely endeavor, which is why I feel so lucky to have a small army to help me along the way. There are the Coco boys and girls of Simon Pulse: Michael, Sangeeta, Jennifer, and Bethany. There is my reading patrol, a clever assortment that includes Heather, Rebecca, Jay, Paul, and Eva. And of course there is my family, without whom none of this would be possible.

# One

Love at first sight is supposed to happen when locking eyes on a busy Parisian street corner or while sharing a booth during a poetry reading at a crowded SoHo coffee shop. It's not supposed to take place while you're on a rooftop in the middle of night spying on a guy like some pathetic perv. Unfortunately, I seem totally incapable of doing anything the way it's supposed to be.

It wasn't technically *first* sight. I had seen Zach countless times before, just never with the roller-coaster drop in my stomach or the sudden shift of cabin pressure in my head. As for the spying, there was no premeditation or intent to stare. (At worst it makes me a second-degree Peeping Tom.)

It happened on New Year's Eve, as the worst year of my life was mercifully coming to a very dull and uneventful end. All of the New Year's essentials like cool music, good friends, and a boyfriend to kiss at midnight were glaringly absent.

It was just me—all alone—on the roof of a decrepit hotel overlooking godforsaken Coconut Beach, Florida. (Okay, "decrepit" and "godforsaken" are a bit harsh, but since this happened a few minutes before my resolution to be less negative and dramatic, I think they're acceptable and appropriate.)

The moment was in stark contrast to the previous New Year's, which I spent at Hadley Montgomery's townhouse on Manhattan's Upper East Side. Had's family is sick rich, and the party was loaded like a Lexus. They had a rocking band and shrimp the size of my head. At midnight, when I kissed my boyfriend, Brendan, I closed my eyes, knowing that my life was perfect. Fast-forward three hundred sixty-five days and my eyes are wide open to a very imperfect world.

It would have been one thing if we had come to Florida on some sort of lame family vacation. At least then it would have been tolerable. I could have acted like I was having a good time while secretly counting the seconds until a flight would carry us back to civilization.

But there would be no flight to catch and no civilization to call home. We were not just staying at the hotel. We had moved in—permanently!

I'll skip the rancid details. Just know that my father had a full-on midlife crisis and somehow convinced my mom to go along for the ride. (Here's the part I didn't get. If it was *his* crisis, why was *I* the one who had to suffer?) He quit his job on Wall Street, cashed out all of his investments, and sold our sweet TriBeCa apartment two blocks from the building where Gisele Bündchen lives. (Not that the two of us hung out or anything, but it was more than a little nice to think we went to the same Starbucks.)

Then he put all of the money together and bought the Seabreeze Hotel. If that sounds glam, believe me, it isn't. The Seabreeze isn't one of those cool hotels in South Beach with Crayola colors and a lobby full of people who look like they're ready for a fashion shoot. It's strictly an old-school wooden dinosaur with guests who are a lot more *America's Funniest Home Videos* than *America's Next Top Model*.

The hotel has two main floors, which stretch along the beach so that each room has an ocean view. The third floor is much smaller and only has five rooms, which connect to form a suite. That's where we live. Officially, it's called the penthouse. (As if.) There's even a PH button instead of a 3 in the elevator. (I like to say the PH stands for "piehole.")

Our place looks kind of like the top tier of a wedding cake. I can step over the railing of my balcony directly onto the roof. I keep an old aluminum beach chair hidden up there, and whenever I want to get away from everything, I can slip out onto the roof and practically disappear. Lately this had been an extremely frequent urge. That's why I was up there on New Year's Eve.

There was a pretty decent-size party going on downstairs in the hotel ballroom. It was a fifty-fifty mix of hotel guests and locals, with a band that played covers of pop songs. I hung tough until they decided to bust out "YMCA." That's when I bolted.

I knew it was lame of me not to stay. (Maybe even lamer than their version of "YMCA.") After all, my mother and little brother had completely turned around, so I was the only one still protesting the move. But I was in no mood to party. I faked an upset stomach to get out of it. There was no way my mom believed me, but she let me come upstairs anyway. I think she'd just gotten tired of trying to convert me.

As I sat back in my chair and looked out at the ocean, I could hear the people two stories below counting down the final seconds of the year. They got louder with each one until the clock struck midnight, and then they all blew on toy horns and yelled, "Happy New Year!"

That's when the guilt kicked in. I considered feigning a miraculous recovery and going back down to the party as part of a whole turning-over-a-new-leaf-in-the-new-year kind of thing. But something on the beach caught my eye.

It looked like a person carrying a large object into the water. I've probably seen way too many episodes of *CSI: Miami*, because my first instinct was that it was someone trying to dump a dead body into the ocean. In truth I couldn't tell what it was. There was a half moon, but it was also really cloudy out, which made it hard to see.

As the clouds drifted across the sky, little bursts of light broke through and let me take a better look. I realized that the person wasn't carrying a body; he was carrying a surfboard. Just like that this guy went from being interestingly criminal to positively idiotic. Only a moron would surf in the middle of the night.

Even without the dead body, I thought about calling the police. It's not against the law to go surfing at night. (Actually, I don't know that. It may very well be.) But I was worried the guy might have had a few too many New Year's cocktails. If he went out into the water drunk, he could easily drown.

But this guy didn't move like he was drunk. In fact he didn't even move like it was nighttime. He glided across the sand and picked up speed as he sprinted through the shallow water, lifting his legs up just high enough to clear the surface. Finally, he slid onto the board and began to paddle out.

I shivered just thinking about how freezing the water must have felt. He was wearing a wet suit, but it only covered his arms down to the biceps and his legs down to the thighs. He didn't seem to mind, though. He never made a noise or acted like it was the slightest bit cold. He just paddled silently out to the swells. When he got there, he sat up on the board with his legs dangling over the sides. He glanced back at the beach just as a cloud shifted, and I was able to get a look at his face. Even though he was out pretty far, I knew it was Zach.

That's why it wasn't first sight. I had seen Zach plenty of times before. He works part-time bussing tables in the hotel dining room. He's pretty cute and extremely quiet. And, as this escapade showed, more than a little weird.

As part of the family, I pitch in to help at the hotel. I wait tables in the dining room three nights a week. In the three months we'd worked together before New Year's

Eve, I don't think Zach and I had spoken for more than a total of ten minutes.

I couldn't figure out what he was doing out there, but for some reason I couldn't stop watching. He was just a dark shadow bobbing up and down on the swells, looking for a wave to catch, and I was mesmerized.

The entire episode seemed insane. Not only was the water freezing, but I assumed that nighttime would be when all of the sharks and other deadly sea creatures come out. Whether that was true or not, Zach obviously wasn't worried. Even from as far away as the hotel roof, I could see that he was smiling and totally enjoying himself. Finally, after a few minutes, a set of three waves started to come at him. He lay out flat on the board and started to paddle back in the same direction as the waves. He floated up and over the first two before finally latching onto the last one.

I have to admit it looked pretty freaking cool in the moonlight as he climbed up onto the board, the top of the wave forming a silvery wash at his feet. Even though it wasn't a particularly big wave, he was able to stay up almost all the way in before finally stepping off into the shallow water.

That was it. He only rode that one wave. When it was over, he got up out of the water and carried his board back onto the beach. A breeze kicked up, strong enough to make the palm trees sway, and for the first time he looked cold.

He unzipped his wet suit and stripped down to a pair of board shorts, shivering as he toweled off. (Here's a fact I had never noticed in his busboy outfit: Zach is kind of ripped.) Once he was all dry, he threw on a T-shirt and carried his board back up toward the hotel parking lot.

This is where the perv gene kicked in. I couldn't stop staring at him. It was one thing when he was on the ocean; I could argue that I was staring at him for safety reasons. But here the only explanation was unbridled hormonal intrigue.

As he reached the streetlight at the edge of the parking lot, he looked right up at me. It was as if he'd known I was there all along. Purely by instinct I pressed myself back into the shadows to hide. I don't know why. It wasn't like I was doing anything wrong—maybe a little weird, but not wrong. For a moment we just held the look. Then he flashed a smile of epic proportions. Perfect white teeth, dazzling even in the darkness. They were impossible to ignore. I smiled back and gave him my best nonchalant wave. Like it was totally normal for me to be on the roof of the hotel and for him to be surfing at midnight on New Year's Eve.

Then he walked out of the light and disappeared into the darkness. It was in that instant that I had the roller-coaster/cabin-pressure effect. I plopped down in my little beach chair for a second and tried to figure out what it all meant. But I didn't have much time to think about it, because I heard the elevator kick into gear. The rear elevator only goes to the third floor, so I knew it had to be my parents or my brother heading up to the piehole. Luckily, like everything else in the hotel the elevator is ancient and slow. I had more than enough time to fold up my chair and climb in through my window.

I jumped right into bed and did my best to look like I was suffering from a raging upset stomach. My mother knew that I wasn't really sick. And she knew that I knew that she knew. But you still have to go through the motions and play out the entire scene. That's just what mothers and daughters do.

After a few moments there was a knock on the door, and I was ready for my performance. I expected my mother to come in and make sure I wasn't goofing off, and I was going to greet her with deep bronchial hacking. But it wasn't Mom. It was my dad.

"How are you feeling, Darby?" Unlike Mom, Dad probably thought I really was sick.

"Better," I said with a faint cough, now feeling very guilty.

"Well, I just wanted to stop by and wish you a happy new year."

"Happy New Year, Dad."

He looked at me for a long moment and then said something totally unexpected. "I did a terrible thing to you, Darby, and I'm sorry. Making you move right before your senior year is unforgivable."

I wanted to scream, *That's right! It's*

*totally, horribly, irrevocably unforgivable!* But a New Year's resolution should last at least more than eleven minutes. Besides, with regard to everything else in my life, my dad has always been great. I looked back into his eyes, which seemed filled with concern.

"It's not unforgivable," I said, trying to make myself believe what I was saying. "I don't understand it, but I can forgive it. In fact, I already have."

He flashed me a big smile, leaned over, and kissed me on the forehead. He lingered for a moment with his cheek against my forehead. That's the way he used to check my temperature when I was little and had a fever. I couldn't tell if he was doing it to see if I was sick, or just to go back to a time before I had become such a drama queen.

When he stood up, I saw that my mom had come into the room behind him. She was obviously pleased with what she had seen and heard. As a result she didn't give me a hard time about the pseudo stomach ailment. She just looked at me and smiled.

"Happy New Year, Darby."

"Happy New Year, Mom."

It was the closest thing we'd had to a tender moment since we came to Florida.

After they left, I just lay there in my bed and tried to make sense of the year that was and get my head around the year that was coming. It may have been starting out in Coconut Beach, but it would end with me going off to college. (By the way, the anxiety of waiting for admissions letters also wasn't doing much to help my general mood.)

I followed my normal nighttime routine and looked at my computer screen as I fell asleep. My screen saver was set to be a slide show from back home in New York, with more than fifty pictures in the loop. There were pictures of me and my best friends during all sorts of capers. There were images of some of my favorite New York landmarks, like the Chrysler Building, Central Park, and the Brooklyn Bridge. And there were a lot of pictures of me and my old boyfriend, Brendan.

The thing that was weird was that Brendan and I had never really broken up. My family moved to Florida, and that was the end of the relationship. There'd been no mention of long-distance romance, so we weren't still a couple. But there'd also never been a final moment. That's why I still had his pictures on my computer.

But when I finally closed my eyes to fall asleep, the last image in my mind was not New York or Brendan. It was Zach looking up at me and flashing that smile. As smiles go, I would classify his as dazzling. It also had a hint of mystery. I didn't know if he was smiling with me or smiling at me. Was he laughing at the fact that he'd caught me looking at him? Or was he saying something else?

# TWO

I kicked off the new year by spending an oh-so-glamorous morning tromping around the beach, trash bag in hand, trying to rack up some of the mandatory volunteer hours I need in order to graduate. (I'll skip the fact that "mandatory volunteer" is a seemingly contradictory term, not unlike "healthy tan" or "very good Céline Dion" album.)

The only thing that made the morning bearable was that I was working with Kate, the one real friend I'd made since we moved to purgatory. Even though she grew up in Florida, Kate has a total Northeast vibe. She can be loud, in your face, and more than a little sarcastic.

She is also off-the-hook funny. Not that she was feeling particularly humorous as I held her hair back for her and she tried to throw up discreetly behind a sand dune. Apparently, her New Year's Eve celebration had been a little more festive than mine, and she was paying the price for it.

"I swear to God, I am never drinking again," she said in between hurls. "At least, not until I'm middle-aged and trapped in an emotionally bankrupt marriage." She punctuated that upbeat prediction with one final retch and blow, expertly making sure she didn't get any on her bleach-white Keds.

"You know," I said in the humorously mocking tone that is a constant of our friendship, "I think it defeats the whole purpose of us cleaning up the beach if you're going to spew vomit all over it."

Even behind her Wayfarers, I could see she was giving me the stink eye. But she didn't say a thing. She just kept still for about thirty seconds until she was satisfied that the heaving was (at least for the moment) completed. Then she stood upright and took a deep breath of the salty ocean air, and the color began returning to her face. She wasn't all there, but she was on the road to recovery.

Not that I let up any.

"Now, would that be an example of situational irony? Or is it irony of fate? I always get those confused." Our AP English teacher had been harping on us all semester about the proper uses of irony.

"First of all," she said, as she kicked a pile of sand to cover up any evidence of her misdeed, "let me remind you that it was not my idea to do this on New Year's Freaking Day. I am here because you didn't want to do it alone."

She let that hang in the air for a guilt-filled moment before she continued. "Secondly, since everything I spewed is biodegradable and harmless to the environment, I would argue that it was not technically ironic. It was simply unfortunate and more than a little repulsive."

With that she flashed her trademark smart-aleck smile, and we continued on our eco-friendly way.

We were working as part of BEACH, a volunteer group whose name stands for Better Environments and Coastal Habitats.

There were nearly twenty of us in matching green and yellow T-shirts cleaning up about a mile and a half of beach. Personally, I think the T-shirts could be a little hipper, but the group as a whole is solid, and I'm glad to be part of it. Just because I might not want to live in Florida doesn't mean I want it to become a tropical trash heap.

Around the next dune Kate and I found a secluded spot that had seen its share of late-night partying. "Very classy," she said as she bagged an empty wine bottle. "Mad Dog 20/20. Methinks there was romance afoot."

"Is it too early to declare that this year officially blows?" I asked as I gingerly picked up a napkin with who-knows-what smeared on it. (Did I forget to mention I was wearing plastic gloves?)

Kate grimaced at the napkin before answering. "Well, a year's pretty long, and you *have* only given it ten hours. You probably need to wait at least an entire day or two before *declaring* that it blows. I think the most you can say right now is that it's *trending* in that direction."

"I don't know about that," I countered.

"We're on slime detail. I think that speaks volumes."

"Yes, but we volunteered for it," she reminded me.

As I considered her argument, Kate reacted to something she saw on the sand.

"Now this also speaks volumes." She used her walking stick to point at some burned-out candles, another empty bottle, and an old pillow. "Apparently, cheap wine can lead to impaired decision making. I think we've uncovered a little love nest."

It took a moment for me to put the pieces together, but when I did, I recoiled. "You don't mean . . ."

Kate just nodded. "I think so."

As much as I tried not to, I couldn't help but picture what might have transpired here. When I did, one nagging question came to mind. "Wouldn't the sand make it really uncomfortable?"

"Happens all the time." Kate said knowingly. "My parents were on the beach when my mom got pregnant with my sister. That's why they named her Sandy."

I stopped cold, totally horrified. "Tell me that you are making that up!"

For a moment Kate was able to keep a straight face, but then—much to my relief—she burst out laughing. "I am. But I had you."

Like I said, off-the-hook funny.

"Let's say we declare this area a bio-hazard zone and move along?" she offered.

"Thank you."

We carefully walked around that dune and continued our search for any litter that might be a little less foul and repulsive.

"Wasn't there some big New Year's resolution about being less dramatic and negative?" Kate asked.

"You don't find that disgusting?"

"No, I'm not talking about two people getting busy in the dunes," she explained. "I'm referring to you writing off an entire year on the very first day. Color me crazy, but wouldn't you say that's a tad negative?"

"Aha," I said, going for my built-in loophole. "It would be negative if I *declared* that the year blows. I only asked if it was *too early* to declare it. Technically, I haven't yet offered either a positive or negative opinion."

Kate stopped walking and glared at

me. For emphasis, she took off her sunglasses and let me look into her squinting, bloodshot eyes. They were a shade that even the paint department at Home Depot couldn't color-match.

"It's lucky that I'm even standing up right now," she informed me. "If you're going to try to get me to follow along with clever wordplay and legal loopholes, you're wasting your time."

"Well, I'll have you know that unlike you, I was not up late last night. And, that's the problem. It's New Year's Day, and instead of sleeping off some epic bash at Hadley Montgomery's house, I'm wide-awake and fully alert, totally capable of sucking in all the beauty and joy of cleaning up after people who did have a good time." I looked back at the biohazard area. "Including some who had a *really* good time."

"Ten hours," she said, punctuating each word with a finger thrust. "Your resolution only lasted ten hours. At least mine's going to do better than that."

"You have a resolution?" I said, hardly believing it.

"Yes, I do," she answered firmly. "And it's a good one."

"This I have to hear."

I momentarily stopped my search for trash and focused my full attention on her. With Kate there was no telling what it might be.

She cleared her throat, as if a crisper voice would make what she said seem official. "This year, I am totally giving up on . . . loser boyfriends. No projects. No head cases. No guys who need rescuing. I am a new woman!"

"There is no way," I said, trying not to laugh too hard. "It's in your DNA."

"No, really," she said with surprising sincerity. "I think I can do it. There's got to be some computer geeky guy who will treat me with kindness and respect. And whose idea of a good time is not drinking Mad Dog 20/20 on the beach."

I had a sudden panic attack. "That wasn't your special sand dune back there, was it?"

"No," she assured me. "But I am familiar with the technique." (She motioned to another sand dune farther down the beach.)

"There are tons of computer geeks who would worship you," I informed her. "The problem is, you're just not interested in them."

"That is a roadblock," she admitted with a thoughtful nod. "But I think I can work around it. That's my resolution, and I'm sticking to it."

"I'll bet one night's tips that you won't make it to the end of January."

"You are so on," she said, offering her hand to seal the deal.

But as I reached to shake it, she pulled it back. "Before I make that bet, I need to ask for a clarification."

"This is going to be the easiest money I ever won," I answered.

"If you go to a New Year's party with a loser guy," she continued, "you're kind of stuck with him at the stroke of midnight. Now, does he count against you in the new year, or is there a little grace period?"

"And I'm the one who's looking for resolution loopholes?"

"At least I'm looking for boys," she shot back at me. "You're so determined to hate Florida you won't give any guy a chance."

This was a common charge from Kate, and up until now it had been hard to dispute. But I thought back to the night before and the mysterious smile that Zach had given me after his midnight ride in the waves. "Let's say, strictly hypothetically, that I was to give a local boy a chance."

Kate stopped cold in her tracks, all traces of hangover miraculously gone. "Who? Who?"

"Hypothetically," I reminded her.

"Hypothetically who?" she demanded.

I knew that once I said it, it would be out there forever. But she was dying to know, and I guess I was dying to talk it out. "Zach Miller."

"Zach Miller!" she exclaimed, a little too loudly for my comfort level. (There were other volunteers nearby, and I didn't feel like they needed to be privy to my rooftop shenanigans.) "You mean the Zach Miller we work with, who's cute and smart?"

"And weird!" I added.

She gave me a perplexed look. "What's weird about Zach Miller?"

"Well, last night, at midnight, instead of partying like any sane and rational person, he went out into shark-infested waters on his surfboard. I'd call that pretty weird."

"And you know this how?"

I paused for a moment before saying it. "Maybe I was sort of spying on him from the roof of my hotel."

"Oh, yes," Kate laughed. "He's the one who's strange. You guys are perfect for each other. Besides, I think he's rocking a little Darby fever. He's always checking you out."

"You're just saying that."

"No, I'm not," she continued. "Did you ever notice that he usually ends up bussing the same tables that you wait? That's so he can talk with you at the end of the night when you split the tips. I'm amazed you haven't picked up on this."

"You are purely delusional," I told her. Although, as I quickly ran through it in my head, I realized that we did usually work the same tables.

"About last night," she said, redirecting the conversation. "Did he see you? Or was this strictly a one-way rooftop stalking situation?"

"He saw me," I answered. "And he smiled. Actually, it was somewhat smoldering."

"Somewhat?" she said unsatisfied.

"Okay," I relented. "Completely smoldering."

"Nice. I like it," she said, loving the dish. "And what did you do?"

"I think I waved a little."

"Was it by chance a smoldering wave?"

"Not so much," I said. "It was more in the 'Hi, neighbor' family of waves."

She shook her head. "Was that all?"

"Then I tried to hide."

Kate considered this for a moment. "Very smooth."

"Actually," I said, correcting myself, "I tried to hide first, and then I waved."

Kate wasn't impressed. "Still, not exactly smooth. So what are you going to do next?"

"I have absolutely no idea."

"Also smooth."

"Well, it just happened," I argued. "I haven't had a lot of time to develop a non-rooftop strategy."

Suddenly, I stopped in mid-discussion, totally distracted by a woman doing one of the strangest things I'd ever seen. She was dragging her Christmas tree across the beach. It was one of those moments in which you wish life had TiVo, so you could pause it for a second and make sure you were seeing what you thought you were seeing.

"That's kind of psycho."

"What?" Kate asked, as if everything were perfectly normal.

"We're spending the morning cleaning up the beach," I reminded her. "And now Mrs. Henderson is dragging her lawn trash out here?"

"Oh, no." Kate laughed as though she were in on a joke I just didn't get. "Everyone brings their Christmas trees down to the beach."

"Any particular reason?" I wondered, still not getting the joke.

"It helps fight erosion," she explained. "If you put the tree on the ocean side of a sand dune, it will catch sand that's blowing by. Pretty soon, the tree disappears and becomes part of the dune. The dune gets bigger and stronger, and your Christmas tree doesn't go to waste. It's a slam dunk, environmentally speaking. There's a dune about a block and a half up that has every Christmas tree from my entire life."

Like everything else about Coconut Beach, this just sounded weird.

"That's kind of spooky," I told her. "I hate to say this, but you people are freaks."

"I hate to say it," she replied, "but you're officially one of us, you freak."

"In zip code only. And the first moment I can do something about that, I am heading back to New York City."

"No, you're not."

"And why is that?"

"Because not only are you now one of the freaks," she said, "you are also in love with a freak."

"Love? Really? One smile and now it's love. That's why I didn't want to tell you. You blow everything out of proportion."

As we took our trash bags back to the drop zone so they could be carried off, my throat began to get a little itchy. That's because I knew that along the way we'd see Zach. (Did I forget to mention that Zach is also part of BEACH?)

We walked along the trail of dead pine needles that had fallen off Mrs. Henderson's Christmas tree. I looked around and noticed that there were in fact other dead trees wedged into the sides of some dunes. Freak City.

Then I saw Zach. He was helping Mrs. Henderson with her tree. Normally, he was quiet and shy, but out here on the beach he seemed different. This was clearly his element.

"This time," Kate whispered, "you might try talking to him."

I nodded. "Good tip."

After he finished helping Mrs. Henderson, he looked up at me and smiled. It was the same smile that I had seen the night before.

"Happy New Year," he called.

"Happy New Year," I replied, and I walked toward him. I was so caught up in the moment, trying to play it cool, that I didn't realize there was a four-foot drop on the edge of the sand dune. After taking only two steps, I careened forward, tumbled down the dune, and came to a stop with a total face plant into the dense, hard sand.

I momentarily considered just never getting up. Eventually, like a dead Christmas tree, I would become part of the dune. In that way I could both hide my shame and help the environment. But I could hear everybody laughing (Kate loudest of all), and I realized I had to put on a brave face.

I stood up and smiled. I tried to wipe the sand off my teeth and ignore the throbbing pain in my nose.

Kate came over and whispered, "Now, would that be an example of situational irony? Or is that irony of fate? I get those confused too."

# Three

"It doesn't look broken," the doctor said as he examined the purple blob formerly known as my button nose. He was shining a tiny flashlight up my nostrils, making me rethink entirely my definition of personal space.

"Are you sure about that?" my mother asked in her calm, *I'm dealing with a crisis now* tone. "Darby's nose has always been bulbous and crooked, but it looks worse than usual."

*Gee, thanks, Mom,* I wanted to scream. *There's nothing like following up the blunt trauma to my face with a little more to my self-esteem.*

"I'm sure," he said in a calming tone. "There's no indication of septal hematoma or epistaxis."

"No bleeding," he explained to me with a whisper. "Besides, I think your nose looks perfect."

Suddenly, I didn't mind quite so much him invading my space. Although it would have been nicer if he'd been one of those heartthrob doctors. (No offense, but if this guy were to walk on to the set of *Grey's Anatomy*, the best nickname he could hope for would be Dr. McLumpy.) Still, he seemed to know what he was doing, and all the diplomas on the wall came from colleges I'd actually heard of.

"Mostly, you're going to have to keep icing it," he said as he finally stood back.

"Lucky for me, I have an industrial-strength ice-making machine in the hallway outside my bedroom," I said. "One of the advantages of living in a hotel."

The good news was that there was no need for any medical treatments or procedures. He told us that everything should heal back normally. The next few days were pretty uneventful, as I was mostly forced to stay home and recuperate. During this time my only real accomplishments were beating all the high scores on the Guitar Hero game my brother got for Christmas and managing to seriously guilt my mother by retelling the "bulbous and crooked" story to anyone who would listen. We eventually negotiated a settlement in which I stopped telling the story in exchange for getting a DSL line in my room.

Unfortunately, my nose was still swollen when Christmas vacation ended and it was time to return to school. Apparently, the fates had determined that it wasn't enough for me to just be the freaky new girl with the New York accent and the all-black wardrobe. Now I was also the girl with the throbbing purple nose and nasal wheeze who had to sit through class with her head tilted back to make sure her breathing passages stayed open.

In other words, school was continuing to play out like the plot of a Stephen King novel. The main difference being that in my horror story the killer dogs and blood-thirsty aliens took the forms of cheerleaders and guidance counselors.

Full disclosure: My first few months at Coconut Beach High had not gone well. My grades were fine, but the social scene was heinous. If you injected me with truth serum, I might admit that much of that was my own fault. I was angry about moving. I missed my friends. And I started off with a bad attitude. But other than Kate, there really weren't a lot of people who went out of their way to make me feel welcome. So you can't pin it all on me.

It had been an extension of my resolution to approach school with a better attitude. I had hoped to make some new friends and salvage the second semester of my senior year. But starting it off with a grape Tootsie Pop growing out of my face certainly wasn't going to make that any easier.

One of the very few cool things about CB High is that seniors are allowed to eat lunch outside in the courtyard. Since I brown-bag it every day, I had managed to make it this far into the year without ever setting foot in the cafeteria. It's my goal to continue that streak on through graduation. Normally I would eat with Kate and a few of her friends. But she was busy making up a Euro history test, and it was too cold for the others, so I was all alone.

I didn't mind one bit.

I pulled up my hoodie to fight the cold and cranked up the volume on my iPod. More than anything music takes me back home. Different songs remind me of the people and places I miss. I just close my eyes and sing along. This is something I typically don't do at school, where it might draw some stares. But today, like I said, the benches were pretty empty.

I was singing along with the White Stripes, thinking about when I went with my three best girlfriends to see them at the Fillmore when I suddenly sensed that I was not alone. I opened my eyes, expecting to see Kate.

But it was Zach.

I hit pause and pulled the headphones out of my ears.

"You've got a really good voice," he said, making me feel totally uncomfortable.

"How long have you been there . . . watching me?" I demanded a little more forcefully than I intended.

He thought about it for a moment and smiled. "What's the matter? You don't like being spied on?"

"Of course not! Nobody likes . . ." Then it dawned on me: He was referring back to me watching him surf on New Year's Eve. (Don't you just hate it when people use stuff you did against you?)

"Actually, I just got here," he said with a laugh. "I only heard a few lines of 'Icky Thump.' But I meant what I said. You really are a good singer."

I must be starved for approval, because when he said it this time, I smiled like a total doofus and thanked him. This completely betrayed the sense of righteous indignation I was angling to project. Then I made it worse by adding, "Well, you really are a good surfer." (As if I have any idea what makes someone good at surfing. As far as I'm concerned, if a shark doesn't eat you, you're good.)

"Is it okay if I sit here on the bench with you?"

That was the first time I realized he was holding his lunch.

"Sure. Have a seat." I felt an odd impulse

to clean up around the bench, like it was somehow mine and he was a guest. He pulled out what appeared to be a turkey sandwich.

"How's your nose?" he asked with genuine-sounding concern. "I noticed you missed a couple of shifts in the dining room."

"Yeah, I took a hiatus. Apparently, the sight of my disgusting purple blob ruins people's appetites."

"It's not disgusting at all," he said, taking a bite as if to show it didn't affect his appetite. "I think it's kind of cool. A badge of honor."

I gave him a disbelieving look.

"Well, if nothing else, at least it matches mine." As he said this, he pointed to a bump on his nose that I had never noticed. "I broke it freshman year."

"Septal hematoma? Epistaxis?" I said, repeating what the doctor had said.

Zach laughed. "I forget the exact terms, but it was something like that."

"Bet you didn't get yours by falling off a sand dune like a total moron."

"Worse," he answered. "I wiped out on

a wave and slammed face-first into my surf-board. A lot of blood in the water. My mother screaming. A total horror movie."

"Let me guess. You were trying to surf in the middle of the night."

"No," he laughed. "I don't surf at night too often. Just on New Year's Eve for luck. What about you? Do you skulk around the roof of the hotel much?"

He earned instant kudos for using "skulk," one of my very favorite words.

"That was the only time," I totally lied, and then quickly tried to change the subject. "So you like the White Stripes?"

"Just because I recognized one of their songs doesn't mean I like them." He laughed as he took another bite of his sandwich. "They're okay."

"Okay? They're incredible," I insisted. "Back home in New York I saw them play at the Fillmore, and they were amazing."

"I don't know." He thought for a moment as he took a sip of his Coke. "Don't you think all their songs sound kind of the same?"

"Yeah, they all sound great. What do you like, that Jack Johnson 'isn't life just one big happy beach party' crap?" (I have an unfortunate habit of turning conversations into arguments.)

"Actually, I do like Jack Johnson a lot, especially when I want to feel mellow."

"Don't you mean feel unconscious? They should play that stuff to knock you out for surgery." (Like I said, it's an unfortunate habit.)

"Actually, my favorite is some guy you've probably never heard of."

This pissed me off. Guys always think that girls are clueless about music.

"Try me," I challenged him. "I know a lot about music."

"Israel Kamakawiwoʻole."

I had absolutely no idea who he was talking about.

"You made that up."

"No, I really didn't," he laughed. "He's great."

"He's Israeli?" I asked, still convinced he was teasing me.

"He's not *from* Israel; his *first name* is Israel," he explained. "He's Hawaiian."

"You like Hawaiian music?"

"I didn't used to," he said. "But during

the summer I shape boards at Hawaiian Rick's. And Rick loves Iz's music. He plays it all the time in the shop. It's really addictive."

"And now you're making up Hawaiian Rick's. What's that?"

He gave me kind of a dumbfounded look. "It's the surf shop about a half mile from your house. Haven't you ever seen it?"

"And you make surfboards there?"

"Some. Just to help with the workload during the summer."

"They're not made in some big factory or something?"

"A lot of them are, but the best ones are made in house. We get the blanks from a factory, though."

He could tell by my expression that I had no idea what a blank was.

"That's a big piece of foam shaped like a surfboard," he explained. "But the shaping, the sanding, and the fiberglass are all done here. We have a little workshop next to the store. I hang out there a lot. You should stop by and I can show you. It's pretty cool."

I was quickly coming to the realization that Zach and I had absolutely nothing in common. (That's the problem with love at first sight. It's followed by reality at second glance.) Things remained quiet for a bit before I took one last stab at a solid conversation starter.

"What colleges have you applied to?" I asked. (It is the one question that seniors get asked nonstop. But I was curious: Where did surfers go to college? University of Hawaii?)

"Florida and Miami, in state," he said. "And out of state Maryland, Washington, and USC."

"Is that the University of South Carolina?" I asked.

"Not quite," he said. "The University of *Southern California*."

"I suppose that's for the good surfing."

"Not really," he said. "It's for the marine biology program. It's pretty cool. The students actually live out on Catalina Island, which is about twenty miles off the coast of Los Angeles. What about you? Where'd you apply?"

"My father made me apply to Florida," I said. "But I'll end up going to NYU, Columbia, Sarah Lawrence, or Vassar."

He gave me an odd look with a crooked little smile. "I can't help but notice that all of those are in New York."

"That's why I picked them. I've got to get back home somehow. New York is the greatest place on earth."

The crooked smile disappeared, and I could tell he didn't agree.

"I'm guessing that you don't like New York."

"It's not my favorite place," he answered.

"But you like it here?" I said, disbelieving. "In this dump of a town?"

"You don't have to take it out on Coconut Beach," he replied. "I completely understand why you love New York. It's just not for me."

"If you don't love New York, that only means that you don't know anything about it. You can't just visit it like a tourist. There's more to it than the Statue of Liberty and the Empire State Building."

(Remember what I said about my tendency to turn conversations into arguments?)

"I could say the same about Coconut Beach," he answered. "Have you really looked around to see what it has to offer?"

"Yeah," I shot back. "And it took me a little under fifteen seconds to see it all."

He looked at me for a few moments and took a deep breath. "I guess we just want to end up on different islands."

"What does that mean?"

"I want to go to Catalina, and you want to go back to Manhattan."

Before it could turn really ugly, the bell rang, and it was time to head to fifth period.

"Just for the record," he said as he got up to leave. "I didn't see it as a tourist. I lived there."

"You lived in New York City?"

"Just for three months, but yeah."

For some reason I didn't believe him. It seemed so random. "Where?" I demanded.

He thought for a moment.

"At 405 East Seventy-third Street." He started to say something and then stopped himself. "I hope your nose feels better. I'll see you at work."

I may have grumbled something as I headed off in the opposite direction for my class. I was only about ten steps away when I was overtaken by Kate.

"So, how'd it go?" she asked.

"What?"

"I've been watching you two for the last ten minutes," she explained. "I didn't want to interrupt."

"You should have," I told her.

She flashed a disappointed look. "What did you guys talk about?"

"I pretty much got all over his case and called him an ignorant idiot."

Kate nodded. "Did I tell you how smooth you are?"

"I think you've mentioned it once or twice."

After school Kate came over to my house to study for an English test on John Steinbeck. She was trying to quiz me on *The Grapes of Wrath*, but I couldn't stop trying to dissect my discussion/argument with Zach.

"Where did Tom Joad meet up with Jim Casy?" she asked, reading from her notebook.

"At 405 East Seventy-third," I answered.

She scrunched up her face. "I'm pretty sure it was in Oklahoma," she replied. "Outside the farm, after Tom was released from prison."

"That's not what I meant—405 East Seventy-third is where Zach claimed he lived," I told her. "He just doesn't strike me as an Upper East Side kind of guy. Not even for three months."

She put down the book. She was frustrated, but she was also a friend, and she could tell I was obsessing.

"I don't know New York," she said. "What's there?"

"I'm not exactly sure," I said, trying to picture the neighborhood in my mind. "I bet it's not even a real address. It's probably his locker combination or something."

"Why don't you Google it?"

"Why?" I asked.

"Google the address and see what pops up. If it's not real, or if it's a restaurant or a Starbucks or something, you know he's full of it. Then maybe we could study for the John Steinbeck test. You know, the one that I need to ace in order to boost my grade."

"That's a great idea," I said, really embracing it. "I'll Google it, and then I can confront him with cold, hard facts."

I went over to my computer—the one

with the new DSL line to it—and Googled the address. When the results came on the screen, I just stared at them, dumb-founded.

"What is it?" she asked.

"I'm sorry, Kate; I can't study right now," I said. "I have to go to Zach's."

"You really are worked up," she said. "Are you going to confront him?"

"No," I said quietly. "I'm going to apologize."

# Four

The temperature flashing on the sign at the Ocean State Bank read forty-seven degrees. That's pretty cold for Florida, but I still didn't mind the five-block walk to Zach's house. I needed a chance to think about what I would say when I saw him.

I had basically accused him of lying to me about living in New York. And then, when he gave me an address, my first assumption was that he had made it up. But he hadn't. I realized that the second I looked it up, because 405 East Seventy-third Street isn't a home, or an apartment building, either. It is the address of the Ronald McDonald House.

In addition to throwing epic parties, every year my friend Hadley's parents host a fundraiser for the Ronald McDonald House. I volunteered to help once and learned that the group gives out-of-town families a place to live if they have a family member who is a cancer patient at a nearby hospital. If Zach lived there for three months, it meant that he'd been through something really bad.

Zach lives at 319 Ocean Drive. It's a little house, but it's nice. It's got a kind of tropical look to it with wooden shutters and a big front porch. I still had no idea what to say to him when I rang the bell. I half expected him to slam the door in my face. Luckily, his mother answered.

"Hello, Mrs. Miller; my name's Darby."

"Of course," she said with a warm smile. "I've seen you over at the hotel. Come on in."

The tropical vibe continues inside the house. It's roomy, and the artwork is all bright and colorful. But the first thing I noticed about the house was that there were family pictures everywhere.

"Are you looking for Zach?"

"Yes, ma'am."

"I think he's on the computer in his room," she said. "Let me get him for you."

When she walked down the hall, a lovable black Lab woke up from the dog bed and slowly stretched out her legs before coming over to check me out. She didn't move like she was in any particular hurry, and her eyes had kind of a milky haze to them.

"What's your name?" I asked as I kneeled down to pet her. If she was a watchdog, she wasn't a very good one. After a couple of sniffs, she just rolled over so I could scratch her belly.

"I see you've met Hannah."

I looked up to see Zach walk into the room.

"She is, without question, the laziest dog in the world," he continued.

"She's great," I replied. "How old is she?"

"Extremely," he joked. "We don't know how old for sure. When we got her at the humane society, she was already pretty big. And we've had her for more than ten years."

"You're just a puppy, aren't you?" I said as I continued to rub her stomach. She must have appreciated the comment, because she kind of gave me a smile.

"It's so funny that you're here," Zach said. "I was just about to burn you a disc."

"Of what?" I asked, totally caught off guard.

"That music I told you about at lunch," he explained. "Israel Kamakawiwo'ole. I thought you might want something different in case you ever get tired of the White Stripes. I was going to bring it to school, but if you've got a second, you can come and get it right now."

Needless to say, this was not what I'd expected. I came there thinking he might slam the door in my face, and instead he was making me a present.

Zach led me to his room, which was chaotic but not health-department awful. There were clothes scattered around as well as stacks of books and paper. He tried to straighten up a little and cleared off a chair for me to sit on.

"Sorry," he said sheepishly. "My mom's always on me about my room being messy."

"Mine too," I answered.

"I just finished putting together the playlist," he said, motioning at the computer. "It'll just take a couple of minutes to burn the CD."

"That's unbelievably nice of you," I answered, still kind of pleasantly stunned.

Suddenly, a thought hit him. "Wait a second. What did you come by for? You need me to cover a shift at work?"

I took a deep breath and just went with it.

"Actually, I came to apologize," I told him. "At lunch today I was rude, and it was completely uncalled for."

"You?" he said. "I was the rude one. That's why I was making the disc for you. It's a peace offering. I came down on your music. I came down on your city. Very uncool."

I went to say something, but I couldn't find the words. Just then he looked at me, and something registered, because his expression changed completely. He closed his eyes for a moment. "You looked up the address didn't you?"

"How'd you know?"

"That look," he said, motioning to me. "I'd recognize it anywhere. That used to be the way that everybody looked at me. It was unfair of me to lay that on you. I'm really sorry."

"It wasn't unfair at all. I was pushing you. I practically demanded you tell me."

I hesitated for a moment, not wanting to cross some line of privacy.

"Can I ask why . . . ?" I had trouble figuring out what to say, but he picked it up for me.

"Why we were living in the Ronald McDonald House?"

I nodded.

"My older brother, Dave, had a brain tumor that he battled for about two years. After he'd been through all the doctors around here and in Miami, he went up to Sloan-Kettering Hospital in New York. It was the summer before my junior year. My mom and I went up to New York to stay with Dave, and my dad stayed home to work. He flew up every other weekend."

I instantly thought of all the family pictures in the living room. I desperately wanted him to tell me that the doctors had miraculously saved his brother. But I knew that wasn't how the story was going to end. He paused for a moment and continued.

"The doctors were great. They did everything they could, but it wasn't enough. We brought him back so he could be home, by the beach." Zach looked at me for a moment, and I wondered if he was going to cry, but he didn't. "He died eight days later."

We sat quietly for almost a minute. So far, I had spied on him from the roof of the hotel, fallen down and practically broken my nose at his feet, treated him like a jerk, and made him relive the most tragic experience of his life. I would have to assume his most natural reaction would be to despise me.

A photograph on his desk caught my eye. It was a picture of a much younger Zach on the beach with a teenager. Both of them were holding surfboards and seemed as happy as could be.

"Is that him?" I asked, pointing at the picture.

Zach looked at it and smiled. "Yep. Big Wave Dave. He was the one great surfer in the family. He's the one who taught me. I told you about breaking my nose. It's because I was trying to ride his longboard, which was much more board than I could handle."

Zach smiled at a memory. "In fact, Dave's the one who invented the tradition of surfing at midnight on New Year's Eve. He told me that if the year starts with you on the ocean, it's got to be a good year."

"I wonder what he would have said about starting the year off on the rooftop."

"Knowing Dave, he probably would have been down with that, too." Zach laughed. "The funny thing is that Dave always wanted to go to New York. He had this old beater Jeep that he used to drive back and forth to college up in Gainesville. He always joked that one summer the two of us would just drive up there.

"When he got sick and I found out that we were going, I bought a New York travel guide. That's how clueless I was to the whole situation. I still thought we might be able to sightsee a little in between treatments. But he was too sick.

"Every day he'd tell me to get out of

the hospital and see something, and I always said that I wanted to wait until he was well enough to go with me. But he wasn't getting any better. So he started tricking me. He'd look through the travel guide and come up with some random question about a place. Something that didn't seem right in the guide. Then he'd send me to investigate. It was always something like going to the Museum of Natural History to see if the T. rex was really as big as the book said.

"I'd go with my little digital camera. Then I'd bring it back and show him the pictures of the place. The next day he'd send me to Times Square or Central Park or wherever, and I'd always come back with pictures. I'd just sit there on his bed and show him the pictures of what I had seen."

I started to cry a little, and it took everything I had in me not to bawl. Then Zach stood up and went over to his door and shut it. The back of the door was covered with his pictures from New York. Many of them looked just like the pictures on my screen saver. They showed every landmark and notable place in the city.

He pointed to one in particular. "That's me at the Museum of Natural History," he explained. "I had someone else take the picture with me in it, so that I could be a visual reference for the dinosaur's actual size."

He looked at the picture for a moment, and when he turned back toward me, he saw the tears in my eyes.

"I'm sorry," he said. "I didn't mean to make you cry."

"I didn't mean to make you relive that story," I said, still wiping the tears from my cheek.

"You didn't," he told me. "I relive that story every day."

"Well, now I understand," I said, trying to regain my composure. "You have every reason to hate New York."

He looked at me and smiled. "No, I don't. I have every reason to hate brain cancer. The only thing New York did was give him one last chance to beat it. I just don't have many good memories there."

"I've got a brother," I said. "And most

of the time he drives me crazy. But I couldn't handle it if the slightest thing happened to him. I don't know how you get over something like that."

"You don't. You learn to deal with it. But you never get over it." He didn't have any emotion in his voice. This was something that he had come to terms with.

The moment was interrupted by the computer, which had finished burning the disc. It gurgled out a couple of beeps, and then the tray slid out with the finished CD.

"Aha," Zach said, no doubt happy to change the mood. "You're in for a real treat. Iz can rock your world."

He popped it into a jewel case and handed it to me.

"You may not like it at first," he warned me. "Just give it a chance and listen with an open mind."

"Like I do everything else," I said with a laugh.

Zach's mom knocked on the door and poked her head into the room. "Darby, would you like to join us for dinner?" She looked at the mess in his room and shook her head. "I promise you that I cook better than Zach cleans up. We're having fish tacos."

"I don't think I've ever had fish tacos," I said, searching my memory.

"Open mind," Zach whispered jokingly.

"Sure, I'd love that. I just have to call my mom and tell her."

"Wow," Mrs. Miller said sarcastically, giving Zach a look. "You mean there's actually a way to communicate with your parents when you're not going to be home when they expect? The new technology is just amazing."

Zach gave her a look, but she just laughed it off.

"It'll be ready in about five minutes."

My mom was thrilled to find out that I was at a friend's house, and she let me stay even though I still had the English test to study for.

Normally, I'm not a fish person, but the tacos were excellent. His mom had made this sweet Caribbean salsa that could easily become addictive. His dad was nice too, quiet but funny.

For the first part of the meal, I couldn't help but think about Zach's brother, Dave. In the kitchen there was a great picture of him and Zach, and I couldn't imagine how they could look at it every day and not break down sobbing.

But about halfway through the meal I just relaxed and enjoyed hanging out with them. They acted like they had known me my whole life and like I belonged there. They teased Zach, and he joked right back.

It occurred to me that in all the times that I had been to my boyfriend Brendan's house, I had never felt like I belonged. It was big and rich and seemed more like a museum than a home. His parents were always polite to me, but I never felt comfortable with them.

Afterward Zach insisted on giving me a ride home. I told him I was fine to walk, but it had gotten dark and colder, and he wouldn't hear of it.

Next to the garage I saw a faded blue Jeep.

"Dave's?" I asked, motioning to it.

Zach nodded. "My dad and I are trying to get it running again."

"Very cool."

Neither of us seemed to know what to say on the ride home. I couldn't help but think about what a drama queen I had been since we'd moved to Coconut Beach. This family had been through an actual tragedy, yet I was the one who moped around in a constant funk.

Zach pulled the car up to the hotel, and for a moment it looked like he was going to kiss me. (This, for the record, would have been completely acceptable.) But he stopped short. He looked at me for a moment and said, "Thanks."

"For what?"

"For coming over and for listening to me talk about Dave."

"Thanks for telling me," I said. "And for introducing me to fish tacos and Hawaiian music."

"You'll love it," he assured me. "Iz rules!"

I got out of the car and headed for the hotel. I didn't know what to make of any of it. I couldn't read Zach and what he thought about me. For that matter I wasn't sure what I thought about him. Part of me really liked him. But another part realized we were very different.

I was in such deep thought that I didn't notice someone waiting for me in the lobby.

"Sure, go over and apologize. Then we can study."

I looked up to see Kate sitting in the lobby next to the complimentary coffee station. I had totally forgotten that I was supposed to call her so we could study for the Steinbeck test.

"I'm sorry," I said, putting my hands up to beg for forgiveness.

"So, did he kiss you? The view from in here was obstructed, and it was too cold to go outside and stare."

"No, he didn't kiss me," I told her, a little disappointed by the fact. "But I no longer hate it here. I'm not saying I've fully changed my opinion, but this place is beginning to grow on me."

As I said it, I was surprised by the fact that it was actually true.

# Five

Over the next few days I began trying to adapt to life in Florida. First of all I started adding color to my traditionally all-black wardrobe. On Tuesday I sported a brown polo that I'd gotten with a gift card at Hollister, and on Wednesday I wore the navy sweater my grandma had sent me for Christmas. (Not exactly a rainbow, but at least I was trying.)

Those, however, were just baby steps compared to the giant leap I took on Thursday when I actually displayed (gasp) school spirit. To be fair, I was alone at the time, so nobody saw.

It happened after school, while I was practicing the fine art of the "locker linger."

That's the ability to stand at your locker for extended periods of time doing absolutely nothing while appearing to be busy. The idea is that you if you stall long enough, you can "accidentally" bump into someone you want to talk to.

I wanted to bump into Zach. Ever since the non-kiss moment when he dropped me off, I had been struggling to figure out if there was anything going on between us. I thought a casual after-school conversation might give me some indication.

I tried all of my best stalling techniques. I rearranged my books and adjusted my hair in the mini mirror taped inside the locker door. I even flipped through my Euro history folder like I was looking for a missing assignment.

But there was no sign of him.

I ran out of things to do in my locker and turned my attention to the hallway. That's when I noticed a banner taped to the wall that read THIS IS CONCH COUNTRY.

A conch (as I discovered on the first day of school) is a type of giant seashell. It is also the name of the mascot at Coconut Beach High.

I'm not joking.

The teams are actually called the Coconut Conchs. Personally, I think that sounds like an appetizer tray at Red Lobster. But that's just me. At games there's even a guy who dresses up in a skintight gold tracksuit and wears a big red shell over his body. Whenever my life seems bad, I imagine the hell that he must go through, and it makes me feel better by comparison.

The apparent lameness of the mascot has done nothing to dampen school spirit, though. Even Kate, whose sarcastic approach to life equals mine, is die-hard. She never misses a home football or basketball game. She's even part of the Conch Heads, a group of fans who bring actual conch shells to the games and blow into them like trumpets when the team needs a surge of support.

I was looking at the banner when a group of kids rushed past on their way to the bus loop. As they hurried, they made a sort of hallway tornado that pulled the front end of the sign loose from the wall. It fluttered in the air for a moment before drooping down to the floor. As it fell, it folded just perfectly so that instead of CONCH COUNTRY all you could read was TRY.

This is where my giant leap occurred. I took the TRY as God's karmic message that I should *try* to have a little school spirit. I put my books into my locker and went over to fix the sign.

I carefully smoothed out the butcher paper and used my hand like an iron to press the masking tape to the wall. I may have considered myself an illegal alien, but I was doing my little part for Conch Country. I even double-checked it to make sure everything looked straight and neat.

When I was done, I went back to my locker and stalled for a little bit longer. I rearranged my books again, this time so that they went in order from first period to last, but there was still no sign of Zach.

"He's not coming."

I turned to see Kate walking toward me.

"Who's not coming?" I stammered, trying to pretend that she hadn't caught me in the act.

"Who?" she echoed skeptically. "You weren't just stalling, hoping to run into someone?"

"How pathetic does that sound?" I asked, hoping that it didn't sound too pathetic. "I was just putting my books away so I could go home."

"Uh-huh," she said, still unconvinced. "Then I guess you're not interested in knowing that Zach checked out in the middle of sixth period for a dentist's appointment."

I sighed and slapped the locker door shut.

"Just what I thought," Kate said. "So, since you've got some spare time now, why don't you come with me to a meeting?"

Now I was the one flashing the skeptical look. "What type of meeting?"

"A *club* meeting. You said that you were going to try to get involved in school. I thought this could be a good first step."

"What club?"

"A *school* club," she said, as if that would be enough. "What does it matter?"

I didn't respond.

She bit her bottom lip for a moment before finally answering. "Okay. The Spirit Club."

"Spirit Club?" I almost gagged. "You can't be serious."

"Well, our school doesn't have a chapter

of the Angry New Yorkers Club. Spirit is the best I can do."

*That's karma for you,* I thought. *Fix one banner and suddenly you've got school spirit.*

"Does it have to be the Spirit Club?" I pleaded. "Isn't there something a little less . . . cheerful?"

"Don't worry," she assured me as she put her arm around my shoulder and started walking me toward the meeting. "You'll make it less cheerful just by walking in the room."

"That really hurts," I joked. "I'll go. But if it gets ugly in there, you'll be the one to blame."

As we walked down the hall, I felt just like I did when I was seven and had to jump off the high dive at the YMCA for the first time.

"I'm not blowing into a conch shell," I declared as we reached the door.

"I wouldn't even think about it," she told me.

As expected, I didn't exactly blend in with the rest of the Spirit Club. Most of them looked like they had been manufactured in some top-secret Abercrombie &

Fitch cloning lab. They all had the same clothes, the same hair, and the same *what the hell are you doing here?* look on their faces.

I made sure to get a seat by the door, just in case there was a little too much spirit and I had to make a run for it. I was so focused on my escape plan that at first I didn't notice that the girl holding the gavel was Monica Baylor.

I don't mean to sound like some delusional superhero, but Monica Baylor is my archnemesis. For some unknown reason she has had it out for me since the first day of school. She talks behind my back, tries to make me look foolish, and always says these little remarks that sound okay but really aren't.

To make matters worse, we work together almost every Friday in the hotel dining room. She's a total brownnose to my parents and has them completely snowed. I can't complain in the slightest without coming across like a complainer.

If I had known she was president of the Spirit Club, I would never have set foot in the room. But by the time I realized it, it was too late to escape. She banged the gavel against the desk and started the meeting.

Right then she noticed me, and a kind of wicked smile came over her. "Well, well, I see we have a new member," she said, motioning to me. "Why don't you stand up and introduce yourself? I'm not sure that everybody has gotten a chance to meet our new friend from the Big Apple." (See what I mean?)

I stood up slowly and flashed a little wave to the others. "Hi, I'm Darby McCray," I said totally hating every second of it. "I'm not officially a member. I'm just kind of seeing what you're all about."

"What we're all about," Monica said, "is Conch spirit!"

Everyone let out a little war whoop, and at that moment I didn't know who I hated more, Monica for being Monica or Kate for bringing me here.

"You picked a great day to come and *see* us," Monica said, "because today we are planning our parade float."

The words "parade float" caused my throat to tighten up. I tried to give Kate a *what have you gotten me into?* look, but she was doing an impressive job of avoiding eye contact of any kind.

"As y'all know," Monica continued, "we really want to show our school spirit and take home the grand prize this year. To do that, we have to absolutely, totally nail the theme."

(Pet-peeve alert: I *absolutely*, *totally* hate it when people use two words that have the same meaning. As if we could *absolutely*, *partially* do something.)

"The theme of this year's parade is . . ." She took a pause for dramatic effect before saying, "Sea of Love!"

Some of the girls in the room actually clapped. Like this was somehow applause-worthy. While they did, I finally managed to put myself in Kate's line of sight.

"Parade?"

"Didn't you know?" she said with a smile. "Every year, Coconut Beach has a big parade on Valentine's Day."

"Parades are for Thanksgiving and Cinco de Mayo. Or when the Yankees win the World Series," I pointed out. "No one has them for Valentine's Day."

"Well, we do," she informed me. "And around here it's a big deal."

I sat back in my chair, stunned. As I was currently without boyfriend and Valentine's Day was fast approaching, I'd been hoping to pretty much ignore it, like I had New Year's. That wouldn't be easy with marching bands and parade floats to remind me.

"Does anyone have any suggestions for the float?" Monica asked, looking around the room. "How about you, Darby? New York has a lot of parades. Do you have any hidden expertise you can share with us?"

She knew that I didn't have the slightest idea what to do for a float. Otherwise she would have never called on me. But I wasn't about to give her the satisfaction.

"Sure," I said, my mind racing for an idea. "It's not expertise, but maybe we could do something with . . ."

I stalled, and she pounced. "With what?"

All that came to mind was the banner. Without even thinking about it, I blurted out, 'This Is Conch Country.'"

There was a moment of quiet in the room, and I kept trying to come up with an explanation.

"Maybe I'm missing something," Monica said. "How does 'This Is Conch Country' translate into a float?"

"Y-you know how, when you put a conch shell up against your ear, you hear the ocean?" I said with a slight stutter.

"Yes," she mocked. "We all know that. We live at the beach."

"If we built a giant conch shell on the float, we could put huge speakers in it, like the kind they have in those cars that vibrate at the stoplight."

Suddenly, I realized that the others were all looking at me. But unlike Monica, they seemed to be actually interested in what I had to say.

"And instead of the ocean, we could have music coming out of it."

Monica could sense the changing tide, but she still tried to sabotage my idea.

"Like what?" she said.

This is where my knowledge of music came to the rescue. "Sea of Love," I answered.

"There's a song called 'Sea of Love'?" she asked and I knew that I had her on the run.

"It's great," I said. "And it's been

recorded by all kinds of artists. We can have the different versions coming out of the conch. It can be rock and country and reggae. That way there'll be something for everyone. It will have the conch—which ties in perfectly for the school. And it will *absolutely*, *totally* nail the theme."

There was a moment of silence as the others considered the pitch.

Kate gave me a look of great surprise. "I like it," she said. A couple more of the girls nodded along and agreed with her. "I like it a lot."

"It's *okay*," Monica said. "But I think I have a better idea." She held up a folder that contained several sheets and diagrams. She had obviously put a lot of thought into her design plan and never really planned to consider anyone else's ideas. But the room seemed to like mine.

"Tell us what it is, Monica," I said, putting the challenge to her. "I'm sure it's great."

Monica flipped through her papers, clearly surprised at the changing tide. "I thought we could have a scene with a mermaid," she said, holding up a picture for all to see. "And the mermaid could be sitting on a throne. So she's 'Under the Sea' and in love."

"You mean like the Disney movie?" someone asked skeptically.

"Not like that," she said, obviously flustered. "It would be much more mature and cutting-edge than that."

This is where Kate swooped in for the kill. "Who's going to play the mermaid?" she asked, knowing full well what the answer had to be.

"Well, as the Spirit Club president," Monica stammered, "I figured that . . . I would probably play the mermaid. Unless someone else wants to do it."

Kate kind of scrunched her face up as she considered the whole thing. She let Monica sway in the breeze for a minute. "I think I like the musical conch shell more."

"Me too," said another girl. And just like that, Monica's idea died a public and painful death. I knew this would only stoke the flames of whatever had caused her to hate me in the first place.

There were a few more suggestions,

but by the end of the meeting my idea had carried the day. And that was just the beginning. Because the hotel has a large parking lot, it was chosen as the building site. With that in mind it seemed only logical that I be put in charge of construction.

Somehow, a girl with no school spirit had been put in charge of the most ridiculously school-spirited thing of all.

"I hold you completely responsible," I said to Kate as we walked home.

"Forget that," Kate said. "I take full credit."

"Credit?!" I exclaimed. "Were you there? That was a horror show."

"Tell me you don't love it," she said. "You know how badly Monica wanted to play out her big mermaid fantasy. And you killed it with your little 'This Is Conch Country.'"

I thought about it for a minute and couldn't resist the urge to smile.

"Okay," I said. "I do love that. But I don't have any school spirit and I'm in charge of the freakin' float."

"Besides," she added, "I wasn't the one

who made you fix the banner when it fell. You already had the Conch spirit in you."

"You saw that?" I demanded.

Kate just laughed. "When are you going to figure it out, Darby? I see everything."

# Six

My dad's idea of the perfect breakfast is a stack of pancakes, maple syrup, sausage links, and buttermilk biscuits. Unfortunately for him, our kitchen is controlled by my mother, a total fitness freak who never misses yoga, runs half marathons, and has banned all of what Dad calls the "fun foods" from the house.

That's why I found him staring down at his sliced grapefruit with the same expression I usually reserve for calculus homework and standardized tests. He poked at it with his fork, but I could tell he had no interest in actually eating it.

"Good morning." I yawned as I slid my backpack onto the table.

He didn't really answer with words. He just kind of grumbled and stabbed at the grapefruit again.

I started digging through the cereal boxes in the pantry. They were all healthy and featured exotic grains and assorted dried fruits. There were no cartoon characters on the boxes, just promises to lower cholesterol and raise fiber content. None of it looked inviting.

"Morning, Darby," he said, as if he had finally noticed I was in the room with him.

"Where's Mom?" I asked, looking over my shoulder.

He gave me a *do you really have to ask?* look.

"Running on the beach," I said, answering my own question.

"She wants to put five miles in this morning," he said, shaking his head. My parents make a great couple. They're really in love. But to the outside world I'm sure they seem like they have nothing in common. He's soft and chubby and is never in too much of a rush. Meanwhile, she can still fit into her prom dress and is always doing three things at once.

"So we're alone?"

"Unless you count the snoring twelve-year-old in the other room," he answered. "But Drew won't be up for at least an hour."

I smiled and pulled out a box of European cereal with a name I couldn't pronounce. I grabbed the milk from the refrigerator and two bowls from the cabinet. I put one of the bowls in front of my father.

"What's that?" he asked with an arched eyebrow.

"Moo . . . lie . . . nexx," I said, trying to pronounce the name as best as I could. "You're obviously not going to eat your grapefruit, so I thought you might like some cereal."

He laughed. "Thanks, but I already had my recommended daily allowance of Styrofoam."

"Dad," I replied, putting a comforting hand on his shoulder. "Aren't you the one who's always saying we need to try new things?"

He didn't really answer, and I took it as a sign he was willing to give it a go. I opened the top and poured the cereal into his bowl. It took a moment for it to register, but his eyes lit up when he looked at the bowl. There may have been health-food markings on the box, but the cereal inside was one of his faves.

"Oh—my goodness," he stammered. "That's Cap'n Crunch!"

I shushed him. "You don't want to wake Drew up. He would totally blab."

"You're right; he would," he said, nodding. "Where did you get that?"

"I bought it at the store and swapped the box."

"It looks so golden and delicious," he said with a broad smile as he doused the cereal with milk. He ate a spoonful and savored it for a moment. "You little outlaw. I don't know if I've ever been so proud of you."

It was over two bowls of bootleg cereal that my father and I spent twenty minutes talking and laughing just like I had always remembered us doing.

He listened intently as I filled him in on the strange turns my life had been taking recently. First of all there was the absurd fact that I was in charge of building a float for the school Spirit Club. When he heard that, he laughed so hard I expected some of the milk to shoot out of his nose. Second, there was the hard-to-pin-down relationship developing between Zach and me. I didn't give him any names or details. I just told him that there might or might not be a boy.

After we'd eaten (and destroyed all evidence of the crime), I grabbed my backpack and headed for the door. Before I could get there, Dad stopped me and gave me a huge hug. He didn't say anything and I didn't say anything, but we both knew what it meant.

I spent a lot of the day thinking about Zach. Sometimes I got the sense that he was kind of into me. But at other times I got the feeling he was completely not interested. For example, when he gave me that ride home and totally seemed like he was going to kiss me—but didn't.

To make matters worse, Zach's feelings weren't the only question mark. I wasn't sure how I felt about him. There had been the kind of lustful moment when I watched him surf on New Year's Eve. And there had been the emotional conversation about his brother. Both of those hinted at interest. But there were also some very hard-to-ignore facts. We seemed to have absolutely nothing in common. He's a full-on beach boy who not only surfs, but even makes surfboards. I'm a city girl who'd much rather catch a cab than a wave. We like different music, different movies, different everything.

There was also the whole karma aspect of our relationship. Whenever the two of us got together, it seemed like I was destined to do something completely embarrassing.

I didn't see him before school or during lunch, but I used my "locker linger" stalling technique to bump into him between fifth and sixth periods.

In my typically obsessive-compulsive way, I analyzed every word or gesture for signs of his true feelings.

"One more class before the weekend," he said as we walked down D Hall. He seemed genuinely happy to see me. (Good sign.)

"Got any big plans?" I asked, open for the suggestion of a date.

"Just chillin'," he said.

I left him plenty of space to add an invitation for me to chill with him, but there was none. (Bad sign.)

"I'm not doing anything either," I offered. (Pathetic sign.)

The warning bell rang just as we reached the end of the hall and had to turn in opposite directions.

"Are you working tonight?" he asked.

"Of course," I answered. "I always get stuck with the Friday night shift."

"Great," he said with a goofy smile. "I'm working too. I'll see you there." (Confusing sign.)

As he walked away, I was as lost as ever. In just a matter of moments I had gotten both interested and non-interested vibes. He totally passed on a golden opportunity to plan something to do together, and he then seemed happy to learn we were going to work the same shift. Arrrgggghhh.

That night, things were dead in the dining room. January is a pretty slow time for the hotel, so there weren't many guests. And since it was cold outside, the locals weren't naturally gravitating toward beachfront dining. Normally, this would be ideal. With fewer customers I'd have more free time to hang out in the kitchen and talk with Zach. (And undoubtedly get more confused.) But once again fate and karma intervened. Since there weren't many customers, I was moved to greeter. Greeting sucks. There are no tips, and you're stuck at the door.

To make matters worse, my evil nemesis, Monica, picked up all of the tables that should have been mine. In the process she also picked up Zach as a busboy. I swear to God, she knew something was maybe almost going on between Zach and me, because all of a sudden she was showing a big-time interest in him. She laughed a bit too hard at his jokes. She slipped in flirt lines and talked about surfing with him. It was pathetic, but there was nothing I could do about it, because I was glued to the greeter's podium.

Kate was the other waitress on duty, and she saw it too. Her tables were pretty dead, so she came over to hang out with me for a sec.

"Look at that," I said, nodding toward them. "She is totally making a move."

Kate nodded in agreement.

I think Monica knew we were looking, because she made a point of brushing up against Zach as she passed him. Then she looked over at us and smiled.

"I just hate her," I said, probably a little louder than I should have.

"If she were a store," Kate said, "she'd be Abercrombie and Bitch."

I gave her a *you can't say that* look, but I couldn't stop from laughing. Or from trying to come up with my own slam.

"If she were a . . ." I tried to come up with anything, but couldn't.

Suddenly, Kate burst out with a laugh. "If she were a musical instrument," she said, barely able to keep it together, "she'd be a whore-Monica."

I totally lost it, and we high-fived. "We have a winner," I said.

Kate went back to her tables, and I thought about how lucky it was that I had met her. To be honest, I already felt closer with Kate than I ever did with any of my friends back home.

From my position at the podium I could see into the lobby and the check-in counter, where my dad was having a heated phone call. He was normally pretty laid-back, but something was obviously stressing him out. When the call was over, he slammed the phone down and beelined straight for the kitchen. There was no one waiting for a table, so I trailed behind him to see what was wrong.

He had been on the phone to the company that supplies our seafood. I didn't hear exactly what it was, but something had gone wrong, and they couldn't make their delivery. Normally that wouldn't be a big deal, especially since we weren't even remotely busy, but there was a wedding scheduled for the next day. In fact the dining room would be closed for the reception. The main dish at the dinner was supposed to be lobster, and now there wasn't going to be any.

After talking to the chef and making a few phone calls, Dad was able to find a seafood distributor that had enough lobster available. The problem was that we'd have to pick it up.

"We can use our truck," the chef said,

referring to an old bakery truck the hotel used for catering. "We just need enough coolers to put the lobster in."

My dad nodded, trying to put the pieces together. "But we need someone to drive it," my dad said. "I can't, because I've got to meet with the parents of the bride to go over all of the last-minute details for tomorrow."

"I can do it, Mr. McCray," Zach offered as he stacked some dirty plates into the dishwasher.

"I appreciate that, Zach," Dad said. "But it's got a really weird gearshift."

"I've driven that truck lots of times," Zach assured him. "Back before you took over the hotel, I helped out on the catering crew. I even have a Class B driver's license."

"Really?" I could tell my dad was desperate.

"It's no problem," Zach said. "It's more fun than cleaning dishes." He smiled, and my dad smiled back.

"That's true. But I wouldn't want you to go alone."

Just then, Monica moved in for the kill. "I could . . ."

She never got to finish. My girl Kate

swooped in like a fighter pilot. "Monica, table six needs you."

"What?" she asked, totally caught off guard.

"They're dying of thirst," Kate said. "They were asking where you were."

Dad motioned with his head for Monica to get back to work, and she was done.

"I'll go, Dad," I said. "I'm not even waiting tables. I'm just greeting."

"Perfect," Dad said, taking a deep breath. "You two go. I'll give you a bonus. Both of you."

I smiled at Kate, and she gave me a wink back. Within seconds Monica was back from table six, but it was too late.

When we got in the truck, my dad handed me some directions that he'd printed off of MapQuest. According to them, it would take just over an hour and a half to drive to the seafood place. That meant we would have at least three hours together alone in the truck.

I slid the big metal door shut and turned toward Zach. We both smiled, and I told myself, *It's now or never. Either you're right for each other or you're not.*

# Seven

It turned out that the hotel's catering truck wasn't exactly the ideal place to have a "get to know you" conversation. First of all, it was incredibly loud. The engine whined, the gears made an odd grinding noise, and the whole thing was so old that every bump in the road caused something to rattle and shake.

The noise, however, was nothing compared to the temperature. So much wind blew through the holes in the floorboard that it was colder inside than out. But I didn't want to seem like one of those girls who always complain, so I decided to make a joke about it.

"If we don't have enough room in the coolers," I offered, "we can just carry the lobsters up here with us. It's certainly cold enough."

I thought it was a good conversation starter—funny and not at all whiny. I was acknowledging the cold, but also letting him know that I was a low-maintenance girl who could roll with the punches.

"Did you say something?" he called back over the racket of the engine.

This wasn't going to be easy.

I tried again. This time I was a little louder and more to the point. "I said it's probably warmer in the ice chests than up here."

"What about the ice chests?" he called back.

We were less than a mile from home, and my patience was already gone.

"It's freaking cold!" I blurted out.

That he heard.

"I'd turn on the heater, but there isn't one."

Lucky me.

Over the next few miles we struggled to hear each other, and I quickly developed an appreciation for what Alaskan sled dogs feel when they're racing. Even though my nose had mostly healed from my fall, the cold was making it throb and hurt.

"I think there may be some jackets in the back," he said, pointing to the door that connected the cab to the rear. "At least there used to be."

I'm not typically one for wearing other people's clothing, but it was only going to get colder, and any jacket sounded pretty good.

"Do you want me to get you one?" I asked, as I tried to stand up and keep my balance.

"No, thanks," he answered. "I'm good."

"Of course you are," I joked. "Your idea of a good time is going into the ocean at midnight on New Year's Eve."

"What's that?" he called back, trying to keep his eye on the road and the conversation at the same time.

"Nothing." (So frustrating.)

I slid the door open and worked my way into the back. I grabbed hold of whatever I could to keep from falling. It was weird to walk around while the truck was moving. I almost ate it twice before I finally got the hang of it. I realized it was the same as walking around a subway car while it was moving.

The entire back of the truck had been remodeled into a miniature kitchen for off-site catering. It was kind of cool, with a stove, a microwave, and even a little sink. Next to the sink I found the jackets.

They weren't quite the parkas I was hoping for. They were white dinner jackets that the service staff wore on the road. I picked the cleanest-looking one and slipped it on. Apparently, it was made for a professional basketball player, because the sleeves hung a good six inches beyond my fingertips. Still, it was better than nothing.

I was already getting better at moving around as I walked back through the door and got into my seat.

"You feeling warmer?" Zach asked.

"And shorter." I held up my arms with the ridiculously long sleeves.

Zach laughed. "Not exactly a custom fit."

I don't know if the engine got quieter, or if our ears adjusted, but pretty soon it seemed much easier for us to talk. I was determined to make polite conversation and resist my natural instinct to turn every discussion into an argument.

"I really like that disc you made for me," I told him. "Israel Kama-whatever-his-name-is."

"Kamakawiwoʻole," he said, sounding as though he had grown up in Maui.

"That's the one," I joked. "I listened to it the other night while I was doing my homework. Very cool."

I could tell he was happy I liked it.

"That's great," he answered. "I've been making a point to listen to some more White Stripes. You were right. They're better than I was giving them credit for."

The small talk continued for a little while until we reached the subject of the upcoming parade. When I said that I was in charge of building the Spirit Club float, he laughed so hard that he almost swerved off the road.

"What's so funny about that?" I asked.

"It just doesn't seem like your thing," he replied.

(He was absolutely right. But that still didn't change the fact that I was offended.)

"It's not like I'm some horrible person," I said, climbing on my soapbox. "Everyone's on my case to embrace my new surroundings, and when I do, all I catch is crap." I left out the fact that the only reason I'd agreed to do it was to stick it to Monica. I thought that would work counter to the sense of outrage I was trying to project.

"I'm sorry," he said. "I didn't mean it that way. I don't think you're horrible. I think you're fantastic. I just don't picture you hanging out with the girls in the Spirit Club."

Don't think for a second that I didn't catch the part where he said I was fantastic. (Very good sign.) I also noticed a fair amount of contempt for the Spirit Club. This gave me a golden opportunity to strike at my nemesis.

"You're not a big fan of the Spirit Club?"

"Not particularly," he said with a laugh. "I think most of them have a little too much spirit. That's all."

"Then I guess that means you don't like Monica?"

It took him a moment to make the mental leap that seemed so obvious to me.

"Monica Baylor?" he asked.

I nodded. "If you don't like the Spirit Club, I imagine you must practically hate her."

"No, I like Monica," he laughed. "She's cool."

"She's the president of the club," I reminded him, a little too forcefully.

"Yeah, but I've known Mon for years. We're good."

*"Mon"?* I wanted to yell. *You've got a pet name for my nemesis?!* (Bad sign.)

I decided not to pursue the Monica angle. At least not for a while. I was trying to create some good momentum for me, and just the mention of Monica was disrupting my mojo. I returned to talking about the parade.

"I don't really get this parade anyway," I pointed out.

"Well, it's not just a parade," he replied. "It's a citywide party."

"But that's what's so strange. Why the obsession with Valentine's Day?"

"The spring-breakers will start arriving at the beginning of March. They're pretty steady until summer starts, and then the families start to come. Basically, the town is overrun by tourists from the first weekend of March until Labor Day. Valentine's is kind of our last chance to do something for the people in town. It's a lot of fun."

"Well, it sounds stupid," I said. (So much for keeping the conversation light and friendly.)

"Wow," he said, shaking his head. "You really hate everything about it here, don't you?"

*Why do I do this? Why do I rant and rave and turn people off?*

"No," I answered. "I don't hate everything."

"Really," he said. "Tell me one thing about Coconut Beach that you like."

I thought about it for a moment and caught him completely off guard.

"I like you."

There was another swerve.

I was out on a limb, but I still had a little wiggle room. It's not like I'd told him I was in love with him. Just that I liked him.

Even though it was dark, I got the

impression that he was blushing. "Well, that's . . . good," he replied, his voice a little shaky. "I really like you."

This was finally getting somewhere.

There was a short silence, and I couldn't tell what was going to happen next. Then he eased the truck off the highway and into a gravel parking lot. I figured he wanted to focus his attention on the conversation without the distraction of driving. We just sat there for a moment and kind of looked at each other.

"Well?" he said, obviously waiting for me to take the first step.

I smiled. "Well, I really like you too," I answered. "I have for a while." I was going further out on that limb.

He smiled. But it wasn't the kind of flirty smile I was hoping for. It was more like the smile someone uses to hold back a laugh.

"I meant, are you ready to load up the truck?"

I looked out the window and saw that we weren't in just any gravel parking lot. This gravel parking lot was in front of a warehouse marked SCHLEGEL'S SEAFOOD.

"This is where we're getting the lobsters, isn't it?"

He nodded. "Yeah."

Like Kate is always telling me, I am so smooth.

"Okay, then," I said, putting on a brave face. "Let's get working."

Even though it was late, the warehouse was busy. A fishing boat had just come in from two weeks at sea, and the workers were icing down the haul. Two huge guys in ski jackets were spreading ice with snow shovels. They scooped some into our coolers and then a woman named Christine helped us carry them back to the lobster tanks.

Up until that point, all my contact with lobsters had involved melted butter and little forks. I had never picked one up. (Certainly not one that was still alive.) But here I was, along with Zach and Christine, sticking my arm into the freezing water and pulling them out one at a time.

"Pick them up by the bodies, not the claws," she warned me. "The claws are banded, but sometimes they break free."

"Good safety tip," I said with a smile.

Despite the smell, the temperature, and

a tinge of guilt knowing these bad boys were about to be eaten at a wedding reception, it was fun.

The flirt volume rose significantly between Zach and me as we brushed up against each other while trying to hold on to the slippery shells. More than ever I was getting an all-systems-go vibe from him.

As we put the lobsters into the coolers, Christine showed us how to cover them up with damp cloths so they wouldn't dehydrate.

Zach showed off a little as we loaded the coolers back onto the truck. They had to be strapped down to the metal floor so they wouldn't slide around during the drive. As he did it, he added some flexing and straining to show that it took a lot of muscle.

"Let me try that," I said, trying to poke at him gently. "That doesn't look so hard."

"Be my guest," he said with a smile as he stepped back. I attached the last one. Unfortunately, it was a lot harder than it looked. Not that I would have admitted that. After a couple of tries, I finally got the strap to click in, and we were ready to go.

The drive back was a lot better than

the drive out. I toyed around with the old radio and was finally able to get a station to come in. The sound was scratchy and the music was all in Spanish, but the mood was definitely festive.

"Let me try this again," I said, clearing my throat. "Tell me all about the Valentine's Day festival. What goes on?"

"You're just going to say it sounds stupid," he said with a laugh.

"No, I won't. I promise. I'm ready to embrace life in Coconut Beach."

"All right," he said. "It starts off with the Big Swim."

"The Big Swim? I love it already."

"Everyone meets down at the beach by the boardwalk. Whoever is brave enough goes down into the water. No wet suits and no wading allowed."

"Really?"

"You gotta get your head wet to count," he explained. "But if you do, you get a cool T-shirt—not to mention some major beach cred."

"That's good," I answered. "I can always use a good T-shirt. And, you know, some cred."

He gave me a skeptical look. "You're going to go in the water? On February fourteenth?"

"Absolutely."

He smiled and nodded. "After the Big Swim, we go to the parade."

"Do we dry off, or just go wet?" I asked, for clarification.

"We dry off," he laughed.

"Sounds kind of wimpy to me," I told him. "But okay."

"Then we have the parade," he continued. "It's cheesy, but kind of fun. It's got marching bands and fire trucks, stuff like that."

"Are there clowns racing around in little go-karts?" I asked.

"You're mocking this."

"No," I assured him, "I'm just trying to figure it all out. Keep going."

"After the parade there's a picnic at the park with hot dogs and hamburgers. And that night there's Cupid's Ball."

"What's Cupid's Ball?" I asked.

"Didn't your dad tell you?"

"What does my dad have to do with it?"

"It's held at the Seabreeze. Everyone

gets together. They get dressed up and have a big dance."

Somewhere between the Big Swim and the romantic dance, this started sounding a lot less dumb and a lot more interesting.

"You're right," I told him. "That sounds like a lot of fun."

For a moment I wondered if he was going to ask me to Cupid's Ball. But, then I had a terrible thought: What if he already had a date?

Before I could find out, we went over a bump, and there was a crashing sound in the back of the truck.

"That sounds bad," he said, trying to look back at it.

"Keep your eye on the road," I told him. "I'll check it out."

I got up and moved to the back of the truck. Apparently, I wasn't as good as I'd thought I was at strapping down the cooler.

"What is it?" he asked.

"One of the ice chests flipped over," I said. "I'll fix it."

The floor was covered with ice, which made it that much more difficult to maneuver. There was also the problem of some lobsters scurrying around with their banded claws in the air.

I only made it a few feet before I stepped on a particularly large piece of ice. My foot went one way, my body another, and I hung in the air for a nanosecond before landing on my butt.

"What was that?" Zach called from the front.

"Just me," I said, laughing. "It's kind of comical back here."

I tried to get up but struggled. The ice just kept making me slide one way or the other.

Zach pulled the truck off to the side of the road to help. He made it about as far as I did before he lost control. He took a couple of flailing steps before lurching forward. Luckily, my leg helped break his fall.

We started sliding around the back of the truck, desperately trying to scoop the ice back in the cooler and grab the runaway lobsters.

"Pick them up by the bodies, not the claws," I reminded him.

One lobster broke free of its band and

took a chunk out of Zach's hand. Another crawled up into the overly long sleeve of the dinner jacket I was wearing. After a few minutes, though, we were able to get a lot of the ice and all of the lobsters back into the cooler.

"I guess I didn't get that strap completely clicked in," I said sheepishly.

Zach just smiled. The two of us sat there for a moment, our backs against a cooler while we caught our breath.

Then he leaned over and gave me a kiss.

I was freezing to death, sitting on some wayward ice in the back of an ancient catering truck, surrounded by the smells of seafood and diesel fuel.

It was perfect.

# Eight

"Tell me what happened," Kate demanded, putting her hands on her hips for emphasis.

I stopped for a moment and looked at her. "I don't know what you're talking about," I said, completely straight-faced.

She gave me the patented Kate look. "Come on. I want to hear all the horny details!"

(This was an ongoing joke between us. We borrowed the line from the movie *Grease*, when the guys are trying to find out about John Travolta's summer lovin' with Olivia Newton-John. Normally, it's what I say to Kate when I want to know about a date with one of her project boys, but this time she was using it on me to find out what happened with Zach.)

"There are no horny details to report," I said, still playing it cool. "We drove the truck to Schlegel's Seafood, loaded up the lobster, and brought it back to the hotel. Pretty boring stuff."

She stood there and gave me a drawn-out glare. "You're lying," she said. "I can tell by the way your eye is twitching."

Reflexively, I reached up to check my eye. "It's not twitching," I told her.

"Yeah, but you wouldn't have checked if you weren't lying. Give it up, girl."

"Okay," I agreed. (Not that it took a whole lot of arm-twisting.)

Kate and I were putting linen covers on chairs for the wedding that was being held that afternoon at the hotel. I kept my voice down so the florists arranging flowers by the door couldn't hear me.

"We left here," I told Kate, "and the truck was loud, so it was hard to get a conversation going. We talked about music, school, the Valentine's Parade."

"Stop right there," Kate interrupted. "I said I want all of the *horny* details. Not all of the *boring* details. Don't give me conversation topics. Give me bodies touching. Lips touching. That sort of thing."

For some reason I blushed, which is totally not like me. "Well. There were some lips touching. And even some bodies touching, for that matter, but only because we slipped on the ice."

"Ice?" she asked her curiosity piqued. "Where did the ice come from?"

"It's complicated," I explained. "There was a cooler. It dumped over. I slipped. He slipped. We ended up lying on top of each other, and next thing you know, we were kissing."

Kate nodded with a huge grin on her face. "Nice. I like it. Now we're getting somewhere. How was the kiss?"

I thought about it for a moment. "I'd say an eight, eight and a half."

"What are you? A gymnastics judge?" She gave me a frustrated look. "Forget numbers. I want adjectives. Wet. Sloppy. Rapturous. You take AP English; use your grown-up words."

I thought about it for a moment. "Stimulating?"

Kate smiled and wagged a finger at me. "'Stimulating' is a start. What else you got?"

"Inspiring," I offered.

Kate shook her head. "'Inspiring' does nothing for me. Try the other direction."

I thought for a moment and then said with a laugh, "How about toe-curling?"

"'Toe-curling' is good," she said, nodding. "'Toe-curling' is real good."

We let that linger in the air for a moment.

"Yeah," I said, pleased with the selection. "I would say 'toe-curling' was accurate."

"Zach Miller gives toe-curling kisses," she announced almost to herself as she pulled a cover over a chair. "I may have to reconsider how I look at him."

"Hey," I told her, "don't get any ideas. He's off-limits to your feminine wiles."

"All you did was kiss," she said. "It's not like you got engaged."

"Kate!"

"I'm joking. You know Zach's way too normal for me."

We both laughed and continued covering chairs for a minute or so. Then Kate looked at me and asked the million-dollar question.

"So what does a toe-curling kiss from Zach Miller actually mean?"

"I wish I knew."

This time I wasn't just being evasive for the fun of it. The truth was that I had no idea. After the kiss, we'd had to get back to the hotel with the lobsters. My dad had been waiting for us. And we'd never really gotten the chance to kind of figure out the real significance. Was it a heat-of-the-moment kind of thing? Or was it something more?

It didn't help that my experience with boys was pretty limited. Other than a few random dates, my only serious boyfriend had been Brendan—and there'd been no way to miss the signals with him.

Brendan believed in the Hollywood version of dating. Everything was a big production. I thought our first date was going to be a simple dinner, but when he picked me up, he arrived in a limo with flowers. (The limo wasn't a rental. It belonged to his family.) From that point on we did everything as a couple, and he always referred to me as his girlfriend. Sometimes he was a little controlling, but there was never any question about where we stood, relationship-wise.

Zach was the opposite. (And not just because he came with a surfboard instead of a limo.) His signals were either subtle or nonexistent. If Brendan was Hollywood, Zach was Off Broadway. Even the kiss, which sure felt like it meant something, had left me kind of twisting in the wind.

I wanted to call him, but I was also trying to play it cool. Finally, I happened to see him in an old familiar place—the ocean.

The weather had changed drastically overnight. I was fast learning that this was a common Florida occurrence. By afternoon it had gotten warm enough that there were half a dozen surfers out on the waves in front of the hotel. I saw them from my balcony and instantly recognized Zach's lime-green surfboard.

I watched him for a while, and at one point I waved, but I don't think he saw me. I wrestled with the idea of going down there to talk with him. I didn't want to seem desperate, but I also didn't want to just sit back and wait for something to happen.

I decided to trust fate. (Typically not a good idea.)

*If he rides the next wave all the way in without falling off,* I told myself, *then I'll walk down there. If he wipes out, I'm going back to my Calc homework.*

I anxiously watched as he passed on a couple of swells before catching a wave. He was off to a great start. He got up quickly on the board and had some really good form. (As if I could tell.) But after a few seconds he started losing his balance. The board shot out from under his feet and straight into the air. His arms waved wildly as he flipped backward into the surf.

Total wipeout.

A half second later I decided that fate could no longer be trusted, and I hurried down to the beach anyway.

(Technically, I took a half second to make the decision and twenty minutes to pick out a pair of tan Roxy shorts with leg ties, a plaid cami tank top, and a short-sleeved fleece to complete the ensemble. Then I hurried down to the beach.)

I didn't exactly know the appropriate surfer-guy-watching technique. So I did a modified *I'm really just down here strolling on the beach enjoying nature* kind of thing.

It was also tricky figuring out where to stand. I wanted to be close enough to see the action, but as the waves came in, I didn't want to get my Nikes all wet.

Luckily, I didn't have to wait long. Zach saw me, and when he rode in on the next wave, he picked up his board and came over to me. He looked really good with the board under one arm and water dripping off his body. Really good. I tried to figure out some adjectives for Kate but kept getting stuck on 'freakin' hot.'

"Hey, Darby, I was about to stop by and see you."

*Stupid fate,* I told myself. *I should have trusted you and waited.*

"Well, I was just out here embracing lovely Coconut Beach," I said, trying to make a joke out of it.

We stood there for a slightly awkward moment as we each tried to figure out what to say.

"I know what we can do," he said with a smile, and I momentarily got excited. "I can borrow a board and teach you how to surf. That would really be embracing life at the beach."

*Gee, I was hoping for a lunch invitation.*

"Dude," I said, affecting a completely lame surfer accent. "I would, but you know, I just ate, and you're not supposed to go in the water for like, you know, thirty minutes after you eat."

(Pathetic, yes, but I believe I've been pretty straightforward about my lack of smoothness.)

"That's too bad," he said, looking disappointed. "The reason I was going to come by was to see if you wanted to get some lunch over at Mama Tacos. But since you've already eaten . . . I guess we can do it another time."

*I officially hate my life.*

I kept my focus, and we made some headway with regard to small talk before my life took another turn for the worse. One of the other surfers came over to us. (I had been too focused on Zach to notice anyone else.) It was none other than my nemesis, Monica Baylor, who of course looked perfect. When she reached us, she struck a pose with her board resting on her hip like she was in a freaking Sheryl Crow video.

"Hey, Darby," she said. "I love that outfit."

(This is the part that guys don't get. My theory is that truly evil sound waves travel at a frequency that boys can't hear. Because to him I'm sure it seemed like she was being nice. But what she was really doing was making an instant comparison between our appearances. And while my outfit was undeniably cute, it was no competition to her hard body dripping with salt water.)

"Thanks," I said. I forced a smile by imagining I was breaking her surfboard over her head.

"I especially like the shoes," she added with a laugh, although I didn't exactly get the joke.

Zach looked down, and he laughed too. Apparently he hadn't noticed the problem before, but luckily she had now pointed it out to him.

"What's so funny about my shoes?" I asked.

"Well, for one," she said, "you're wearing them on the beach."

I looked to Zach for guidance.

"Most people go barefoot or wear slaps," he said. ("Slaps," I figured out, is what beach people call flip-flops.)

"Oh, I know that," I said with a laugh, trying to cover. "I only have them on because I was about to go for a run. But then I saw Zach and wanted to say hello."

Monica knew I was full of it, but Zach seemed to buy it, and for the moment that was all I was worried about.

Monica turned to Zach, like I wasn't even there. "Some of the guys are going to head over to Mama Tacos, if you want to come."

"Sure," Zach said. Then he turned to me. "I know you've already eaten. But, would you like to join us?"

*"Us"?* I thought. *No, I would like to join you.*

"Sure, you could come too," Monica said, as though it had just occurred to her that I was also allowed to go to Mama Tacos. "But I know you're about to go running. And Mexican food and running aren't exactly a perfect match."

"That's right," Zach remembered. "I forgot about the running."

"Maybe next time," I said, conceding defeat for the moment.

To make matters worse, since it was going to take a few moments for all of them to wipe down the surfboards, I had to actually go running on the beach.

(Unlike my mother, I don't think of running as time well spent.)

As I jogged down the beach, I realized that I needed to change my plan of attack. Especially with Monica hovering around the picture. I couldn't just wait for Zach to make the next move. I was going to have to take charge.

I quickly began to formulate a plan, which I put in motion that afternoon, when I walked over to Zach's house. He and his dad were in the driveway, working on the old Jeep that had belonged to his brother, Dave. Mr. Miller had the hood up and was doing something to the engine. Zach was in the driver's seat.

"Give it a little more," his dad called out.

Zach pressed on the gas, and the engine revved. When he looked up and saw me, he smiled. I smiled back and waved.

"Hey," I shouted over the engine noise.

"Hey," he called back.

"And more," his dad instructed, his head still under the hood.

Zach revved the engine again. I couldn't quite tell what his father was doing, but it must have worked, because when he stepped back from the engine, he had a big smile on his face.

"Sounds good," he said. Then he noticed me. "Hiya, Darby."

"Hi, Mr. Miller," I answered. "How's the Jeep coming?"

"She should be running by tomorrow."

I smiled. "Excellent news."

He turned to Zach. "Where are those spark plugs?"

"In the garage."

"I'll be right back."

Mr. Miller went to the garage, but I kind of got the impression he was trying to give us a few minutes alone, which I thought was pretty cool.

Zach got out of the Jeep and motioned to the driver's seat. "Why don't you check it out?"

I climbed up behind the wheel and settled down into the seat a little. The Jeep was a little ragged from age, but it had tons of character. The more I sat there, the more I liked it. I reflexively reached down to the gearshift.

"Do you know how to drive a stick?" Zach asked.

"Not exactly." I gave him a sheepish smile. "I'm sure you're going to laugh when I tell you this, but I don't know how to drive any kind of car."

Zach gave me a bug-eyed look. "You're serious?"

This is the thing that people who aren't from New York don't realize. The only drawback of growing up in Manhattan is that you never get a chance to drive. Never.

"Back home my family didn't even have a car," I explained. "That's city life. You walk, ride the subway, or take a taxi. Hardly any of my friends have licenses."

"You know, I never thought about it, but that makes total sense," Zach said. "One day maybe I can show you how to drive it. That would be fun. Possibly terrifying, but fun."

"Actually," I said, turning to the plan I

had laid out before coming, "I was hoping you might be able to show me something else."

"What's that?"

"Coconut Beach," I answered.

Zach gave me a slightly confused look. "What do you mean?"

"You have pointed out, rightfully so, that I haven't really explored the area as much as I should have," I explained. "Maybe I've misjudged it. I want you to show me why you think it's great."

"I could do that," Zach answered, quickly warming up to the idea. "I could be kind of like your spirit guide."

"Exactly."

(Okay, so "spirit guide" wasn't exactly "boyfriend," but at least it was something. And anything that put us together might also create the opportunity for another toe-curling kiss, and I was all for that.)

"When do we start?" he asked.

"When do you have time?"

He thought for a second. "My dad and I will be working on the Jeep for the rest of the day. What are you doing tomorrow?"

"I'm totally open," I said hopefully.

"And you mean it? You really want to get to know the beach?"

I nodded. "Absolutely."

"Great," he said. "I'll pick you up tomorrow morning at nine . . . in the Jeep. It should be ready by then. We'll make a day of it."

"Perfect."

(Actually, nine in the morning sounded a bit early for my taste, but a day tooling around on the beach in a Jeep sounded great. In fact, it sounded an awful lot like a date.)

"And, oh," he added, "bring your brother."

(Or maybe not so much a date.)

# Nine

My brother, Drew, was born the day I turned five, and I swear he did it just to ruin my birthday party. Even though she wasn't due for another two weeks, my mother's water broke right as I went to blow out the candles on my cake. (Not exactly what I was wishing for.) In other words Drew has been in my way since the moment he was born. And now, for reasons I didn't quite understand, he was tagging along on what I had hoped was going to be a date with Zach.

If I was less than thrilled to bring my brother, my parents were ecstatic about it. Mom practically cried when I told her Zach and I were taking Drew out. (Realizing a chance for some much-needed suck-up points, I acted like it had been my idea all along.)

But as we waited for Zach in the hotel lobby, I was already thinking it was a mistake.

"What do you think you're doing?" I demanded as he poured himself a cup of coffee.

"The sign says complimentary," he responded. "That means it's free."

"Free to grown-ups and guests," I said, taking the cup from his hand. "You're not supposed to drink coffee."

"And you're not supposed to sneak around on the roof," he said, snatching the cup back from me. "Didn't think I knew about that, did you?"

Actually, I hadn't. But I played it cool.

"Fine, drink it; stunt your growth," I told him. "I don't care. Those are Mom and Dad's rules. You can deal with them."

He smiled and took a sip. It was obviously stronger than he expected, because he gagged a couple of times. But he was playing things cool too, and he acted like it was no big deal. He started opening up little packets of sugar and pouring them in his cup. A lot of them.

"My rules, however, are a different matter. Let's go over them before he gets here." I looked down at Drew, trying my best to seem menacing.

He continued to shake in more sugar. "I know the rules."

"Good. Then let me hear them."

He listed them, using that little smart-aleck voice that drives me crazy. "No barf jokes. No nose-picking. No pulling my underwear out of my butt."

He tried another sip and gagged again. Even with a pound of sugar in it, the coffee was still too strong.

"And . . ."

He rolled his eyes. "And . . . no using the word 'boyfriend.'"

"Good," I said. "Follow those rules and you'll get your twenty bucks."

Just then Zach pulled up in the Jeep.

"He's here. Play it cool."

Drew's idea of playing it cool was bursting through the door at full speed and shouting, "Cool Jeep! I call shotgun!"

"You can't call shotgun," I tried to say, but it was too late. Before I could do anything to stop him, Drew was in the passenger seat with his seat belt clicked.

Normally, I would have whacked him in the head and made him move to the back. But, I was trying to make a good impression on Zach, so I just let it go.

"Congrats on getting the Jeep running," I said to Zach as I climbed into the backseat.

"For now at least," he said. "We'll see how far it goes."

"Zach, this is my brother, Drew. Drew, this is Zach."

Zach smiled, and Drew jammed his finger up his right nostril, dug in for some long-lost booger, and asked, "Are you my sister's boyfriend?"

Zach struggled to find the right response, so I came to his rescue. "Just ignore him," I explained. "It makes life easier."

I gave Drew the stink eye, and he looked back at me and mouthed, "I don't need twenty dollars." This was going to be an adventure for sure.

As we pulled away from the hotel, I

noticed that the stereo was playing a White Stripes song. I didn't know if Zach had put in a CD or if the song was just randomly on the radio, but I took it as a good sign.

Despite the preteen fart machine in the front seat, riding in the Jeep was pretty boss. Of course I would have preferred for it to be the two of us, but I decided to make the most of it.

"So, where are we going?" I asked.

Zach looked at me in the rearview mirror and smiled. "To one of my favorite places in the world."

I went to say something, but Drew decided he had a pressing question to ask. "What do you call it when an astronomer barfs?"

Zach smiled. "I don't know. What do you call it?"

"Halley's Vomit."

(From a humor standpoint that was the high point of the trip.)

Drew continued to demonstrate his encyclopedic knowledge of gross-out jokes as we drove along A1A for about five miles. He also spent a solid three minutes trying to dig his underwear out of his butt (thus completing the grand slam of things I had begged him not to do).

At a stoplight I leaned forward and whispered into Zach's ear, "I'm sorry about my little brother."

"Don't be," he laughed. "Remember, I was a little brother too."

Finally, Zach pulled off the highway and onto a dirt road. The Jeep bounced up and down for a couple of blocks until we pulled into a little lot behind a two-story brick building. It looked like a small school.

"This is it," Zach said as he got out of the driver's seat. "I hope you like it."

Drew gave me a look and asked, "Like what?"

All I could do was shrug. I had absolutely no idea what we were going to do.

Zach led us around to the front of the building, where there were about thirty kids being dropped off by their parents. The kids were a little bit younger than Drew—most about ten years old. They carried bag lunches and milk jugs with the tops cut off of them. When one group of kids saw Zach, they went nuts and started calling to him.

"Z-man! Zach! Mr. Z!"

They surrounded him, and it seemed like each one just had to get a high five. It was only then that I noticed that the word STAFF was written in big block letters across the back of Zach's light-blue T-shirt. On the front was a logo that matched the logo on the front of the building.

It said MARINE SCIENCE CENTER.

"Hit the classroom, guys," Zach instructed the kids. "We've got guests, and I expect good behavior."

The kids were well-trained, because after a few more celebratory high fives they went right up the front stairs and beelined to the classroom. Zach turned to Drew.

"I know they're younger than you," he said, "but if you give it a try, I think you'll have a really good time."

Drew looked a tad skeptical. After all, he was a coffee drinker who could fart on demand. What was he going to do with a bunch of ten-year-old babies?

"Besides, you'll get to pet a shark. And if you're good, I'll let you tell five barf jokes."

"To the entire class?"

"Every one of them."

Drew's eyes lit up. "Cool!" He followed the kids to the classroom, leaving Zach and me at the front door of the building.

"Want to tell me what's going on?" I asked.

Zach smiled and gave me his best pitch. "This is the Marine Science Center. It's run by the school district, and every fifth grader in the county comes through here. I thought you could be my assistant for the morning—have some fun and maybe learn a little bit about Coconut Beach."

"Do I have to call you Mr. Zach?"

"No," he said. "Professor Z will be fine."

I slugged him in the shoulder, and he laughed. "Do I get one of those cool T-shirts?"

He reached into his backpack, pulled one out, and handed it to me. "Brand-new. There's a restroom to the right where you can change."

The next two and a half hours were amazing. Zach taught the kids (and me) all about marine life. He was really great with them, and it was a side of him I'd never seen.

We learned about different types of sea creatures and pretended to swim around the classroom like giant octopi. There was a PowerPoint set to reggae music that identified various seashells, and we even did a funny rap song he wrote about how the gravity of the moon affects the tides.

The coolest part was when we went into a room filled with different tanks and aquariums. The smell took a little getting used to, but the aquariums were happening. There were a couple of tanks set low enough that the kids could reach in and touch the sea anemones and starfish. There was even a baby nurse shark in one. Zach had Drew reach in and feel its skin and then describe it to the other kids.

"It's gross and scaly," Drew said. "Just like my sister's face."

"You got anything poisonous he can pet?" I whispered to Zach.

During lunch I was given the honor of selecting the best milk jug. The jugs were meant to carry seashells, and the kids had decorated them with Magic Markers. Some had schools of fish swimming across them; others had drawings of shells. I picked one that had been made to look like a giant shark, with the cut-out portion as its wide-open jaws.

Afterward we all went down to the beach and looked for seashells. Zach and I walked behind them so that he could keep an eye on everything.

"So this is your favorite place?"

"One of them," he said. "I came here on a field trip in fifth grade and instantly knew I wanted to be a marine biologist."

"And you've never changed your mind?"

"Not once." He stopped and made a circle in the sand with his toe. "Do you see the shark's tooth?"

I looked hard. Even with the circle narrowing it down, I couldn't find the shark's tooth among all the tiny shells in the sand.

"How often do you work here?"

"I volunteer a couple Sundays every month," he answered. "It's fun."

When it became apparent that I still couldn't find the shark's tooth, he pointed at it with his big toe, and I finally saw it. I picked it up and tossed it into the jug we were sharing.

I wanted to hold his hand. (Actually, I

wanted to kiss him.) The only problem was that we were surrounded by screaming ten-year-olds and my big-mouthed brother. The most I could do was a little eye-flirting. Luckily, I am an all-star when it comes to eye-flirting.)

After the science center we drove back to the hotel, and my brother hopped out of the Jeep with his jug full of shells. "I had a really good time," he said, in a rare display of polite behavior. "Sorry about all the nose-picking and bad jokes."

"No problem," Zach said with a wink. "Answer this: If you're American when you're drinking a glass of water, what are you in the bathroom?"

Drew's eyes lit up. "I don't know."

Zach smiled and said, "You're a-peein'."

Drew laughed hard and rushed inside, undoubtedly to tell the joke to whichever parent was unlucky enough to open the door.

Zach turned to me. "Are you done, or do you still have more left in you?"

"You're the spirit guide," I answered.

"Great. I know just the place."

He drove me over to Hawaiian Rick's,

the surf shop he'd told me about before. It was my first-ever surf shop, so I didn't know what to expect. The store is in what used to be a little beach house, and it still has a homey feeling.

We walked in the front door and ran smack into a huge man with a friendly smile, long black hair, and an armful of Polynesian tattoos.

"Zach Attack," he said, greeting Zach with yet another nickname. "Who's the *wahine*?" (Later I found out that *wahine* is Hawaiian for "girl.")

"This is Darby," Zach said. "I'm teaching her beach living."

"That's the only kind," Rick assured me. "Why don't you take her into the boardroom and show her your sticks?"

"Your what?" I asked.

"Sticks," Zach told me. "Surfboards."

The boardroom is where they keep all the surfboards made in the garage behind the shop. There were three on display that Zach had made himself. Each had a little *Z* logo near the nose.

"I like it," I said, running my hand along the surface.

"That's called the deck," Zach explained. "It can't be flat, but it has to be smooth. It has to have a flow to it. It takes a while to learn how to shape it."

"And you built this?" I asked.

Zach nodded, a little proud and a little embarrassed at the attention.

"You know, we're looking for some help on our parade float," I told him. "I imagine a boy who can build a stick like this could come in handy."

Zach blushed a bit. "It's not really my—"

"You like how I worked 'stick' into the conversation?" I said. "I'm paying attention."

"That's great," he said. "But parade floats aren't really my thing."

"Maybe because you've never tried it," I said. "I could be your parade-float spirit guide."

"Let me show you the rest of the store," he said, changing the subject.

Three rooms that had been bedrooms when the building was a house were now filled with clothing. One had mostly T-shirts, another had swimsuits, and the final had a sign that said LOCALS ONLY.

"Not very friendly," I said, pointing at the sign.

"Rick's got some rules," Zach explained. "He likes tourists and treats them right. He'll put them on a righteous board and get them some good clothes. But some of the merchandise is reserved for Coco boys and girls only."

"Coco boys and girls?"

Zach laughed. "That's what the locals are called."

"Really? I didn't know that."

"That's because until now you didn't want to be one."

"But I won't really be one until I can find a shark's tooth by myself."

He laughed. "I can help you until you get the hang of it. But you really should find yourself a good Coco Girl shirt. I think it's the next step in your evolution."

I looked at the clothes on the rack. Their bright colors were certainly outside of my wardrobe comfort zone. But I did find a shirt that I fell in love with. It was faded green with a square neck and eyelet trim. It had a tent body and cute little pockets. I held it up in front of me and checked it out in the mirror.

"That is what I call a Coco Girl shirt," Zach said approvingly. "Excellent choice."

I took the shirt to the register at the front of the store and handed it to Hawaiian Rick, who gave me a skeptical look.

"She's local," Zach assured him.

Rick raised an eyebrow. "Are you sure?"

"I live at the Seabreeze," I explained.

"Just 'cause your address says you live here doesn't make you local. Why don't you prove it to me?"

Zach could tell I was starting to get a little pissed.

"Just put up with it," he whispered. "It's worth it."

I tried to think of a way to prove my beach cred and remembered the lesson from the Marine Science Center. "I can name fifteen different types of shells and describe how a starfish regenerates lost limbs."

Rick nodded. "That's sounds pretty local," he said with a smile.

Then I noticed something on the wall behind him. It was a picture of a giant

Hawaiian man who looked like he weighed more than four hundred pounds.

"And I can tell you who that is," I said, pointing at the picture.

"You can?"

I could, because the same picture popped up on my iTunes every time I played the music Zach had given me. "It's Israel Kamakawiwoʻole." (Oh, by the way, I nailed the pronunciation.)

Hawaiian Rick laughed. "She's good *wahine*, Zach," he said as he rang up the sale on the register. "That'll be two dollars, Coco Girl."

"It can't just be two dollars," I said.

"With those answers, it's two dollars," he said with a big smile. "Welcome to the beach."

I smiled back, gave him two bucks, and took the shirt. Then I noticed something else on the wall.

"What does that mean?" I asked, pointing at the words *Mau Loa*.

"'Forever,'" Rick told me. "It's for these people who are gone but live in our hearts. This is my wall of legends."

The picture of Iz was in the middle, but

there were some other ones around it.

Rick pointed to one of a handsome Hawaiian man in an old-style bathing suit. "This is the Duke," he said. "Duke Kahanamoku, the father of surfing." He pointed to one other man with a surfboard. "This is Eddie Aikau, legendary surfer and North Shore lifeguard." And finally he pointed to the last picture. This was the only one who wasn't Hawaiian, and after a moment of looking at it I recognized the face, too.

"And that's Zach's brother," I said.

Hawaiian Rick nodded and took a moment before saying anything. "Big Wave Dave. Best Coco Boy ever."

I looked over at Zach, and he was smiling proudly in agreement.

As we drove home, Zach seemed to have something on his mind, and it took a couple of blocks for him to get it out.

"Do you think you could get off of work on Friday night?"

"I think so. Why?"

He paused for a few moments. "There's this place called Rico's Fish Camp. And they do a special thing on Friday nights.

I thought you might like to go."

"Is that the next step in my beach evolution?"

"It could be," he said. "But I was kind of hoping it could be . . . more like a date."

There it was—the magic word.

"A date?" I said reflexively.

"If that's weird or you're not interested, I completely understand."

I took a quick breath and tried to keep my cool. "I don't have to bring my brother, do I?"

He laughed. "No. It would just be the two of us . . . you know, and all of the other people at the fish camp."

"But we'd be at a table alone?"

He nodded. "That's the idea."

I savored it for a moment. "I like that idea. I like it a lot."

# Ten

I don't know if it was the visit to the surf shop or the fact that I was wearing my new Coco Girl shirt, but I had a Jack Johnson song stuck in my head as I went through my locker before school. Strangely, it seemed to fit my mood perfectly. I had a kind of mellow Zen thing going. At least I did until Kate came along.

"Did they move St. Patrick's Day?" she asked. "Did I miss a memo?"

I rolled my eyes. "Yes, Kate. I'm wearing a green shirt."

"Thank God," she said in mock terror. "I was worried my vision was going."

"Are you finished?"

She thought about it for a moment. "It's too soon to tell," she explained. "What am I to make of this daring flash of color?"

I struck a subtle modeling pose. "I picked it out with Zach at a place called Hawaiian Rick's."

Kate clutched her chest as if she were having a heart attack. "Zach . . . shirt . . . Hawaiian Rick's . . . I feel the big one coming on."

I gave her a little bump as I shut my locker. "Do you mind not drawing so much attention to me? I already feel kind of . . . out there, with the shirt," I said as I started off toward first period. "Do you like it?"

"Yes!" she exclaimed. "It opens up a whole new palette of non-funeral-appropriate clothing for you. This is huge."

"If you think that's huge . . . ," I said.

"What?" she asked with sudden interest. "Is there something bigger?"

"That depends. You know how you didn't have to work this Friday night?"

"Yeah."

"How'd you like to?"

It took a moment for the pieces to come

together for her, but when her eyes lit up, I could tell she had figured it out. "Are you . . . ?"

"Uh-huh."

"With . . . ?"

"Yep."

She stopped cold in her tracks and caused a minor C Hall traffic jam. "Did he call it a date?"

I nodded, and she clutched her chest again. "I really do think this may be the big one."

I gave her my *enough already* look and she straightened out. "Now, will you cover for me or not?"

"Yeah, yeah," she said. "Of course I will. Tell me all about it. Where are you going? What are you going to wear?"

Before I could even answer, the warning bell rang, and we had to bolt to our classes.

"I'll tell you all about it at lunch," I promised.

"Adjectives," she called out as she hurried down the hall. "I'll want adjectives."

As it turned out, I wasn't able to give her any details—adjective or otherwise—at lunch, because Zach came outside and joined us at our bench.

"You guys mind if I eat with you?" he asked.

Kate noticed he was carrying a ziplock bag filled with Girl Scout cookies. "That depends. Are you gonna share those Thin Mints?"

He laughed. "Sure."

"Then we don't mind at all."

I slid over to make room, and he sat down next to me. He proceeded to devour an impressive assortment of food. In addition to the Girl Scout cookies, he polished off two salami sandwiches, a bag of Doritos, a package of string cheese, an apple, a box of raisins, and a can of Dr Pepper. (He obviously didn't have my mom packing his lunch.)

When he finally popped the last raisin in his mouth, Kate looked at him in stunned amazement. "Is that all?" she asked. "Or are they cooking up a side of beef for you in the cafeteria?"

"That's it," he said with a satisfied smile. "It should hold me over until I get home for my after-school snack."

"Good," she joked. "'Cause I'd hate for you to go hungry."

"Well, if you've got any extra celery or another sandwich . . . ," he said, reaching toward her lunch.

"I do not," Kate said, slapping his hand. "You better protect your food, Darby."

"There's no need," I said, holding up a baggie with some puffed potato and rice snacks that my mom had packed for me. "You can have as many of these as you want."

He took one and held it up high to examine it. "What is it?"

"I have no idea. But I do know it has zero calories and even less taste."

Zach shrugged and started eating it anyway. Kate and I shared a look. He was an eating machine. We watched for a moment, and then I had an idea.

"You know, this Saturday we're having a big work day for our parade float," I mentioned. "We're always looking for volunteers to help."

Zach didn't answer. He just kept chewing . . . and chewing. The fact that the snack had no taste wasn't slowing him down in the least bit.

"You know," Kate said, "she mentioned the work day and the volunteers because she was hoping you'd jump in with an offer to help." To further illustrate the point, Kate made a jumping-in motion with her hands.

Zach smiled. "Yeah, I got that. Did you notice how I didn't offer?"

"Yeah," Kate nodded. "We got that."

"Come on, Zach," I pleaded. "Those surfboards you made are great. And the work you've done with your Jeep. We could really use someone who's good with his hands."

Kate went to crack what undoubtedly would have been a sex joke, but I shot her a look. Amazingly, she held back.

"I'm sorry," Zach said. "But spirit clubs and parade floats just aren't my thing."

"That's interesting," I said. "For someone who keeps telling me to try new things, that sure sounds close-minded."

"Nice try, but . . ."

"Seems like a double standard to me," Kate added. "Darby's trying all sorts of new stuff."

I nodded and gave him my best guilt look.

"I offered to teach her how to surf and she said no."

"That was just one time," I pleaded.

He gave me a look. "Oh, okay. Then will you let me teach you how to surf?"

"Absolutely not!" I exclaimed.

"See," he said, pointing a finger like a five-year-old. "What surfing is to Darby, parade floats are to me."

"You're talking apples and oranges," I argued. "It's totally different."

"Different only because you don't want to try it," he shot back at me.

"What if she did?" Kate offered.

"What if she did what?" Zach and I said at the same time.

Kate flashed a devilish smile. "What if Darby were willing to take surfing lessons? Would you help us with the float?"

Zach thought about it for a moment. "Now, that's an interesting concept."

"Hello," I tried to interrupt. "I am here, you know. I can speak for myself."

They both just ignored me. "That does sound fair," Zach added.

"No it doesn't!" I interjected. "It doesn't sound fair at all!"

"Deal," Kate responded, and the two of them shook on it.

"Do you know how cold that water is?" I proclaimed, waving my hands in protest. "I am not surfing."

"You have to," Kate answered. "I gave my word."

"Yeah," Zach laughed. "We shook on it."

I went to argue but realized it was pointless. No matter what I said, they would just railroad me into it. Still, I mulled it over a bit before officially giving in.

"You better really help with that float," I insisted. "I'm talking major construction."

Zach and Kate smiled, and we all laughed.

"I'm going to freeze my butt off, you know?"

They both nodded, and that's the way it was for the rest of lunch. The three of us just kind of chilled and joked around. Normally, I get a little freaked out when I'm around a guy I like, but it felt totally comfortable. (I think it helped that Kate is so cool.) For the first time I really felt like I fit in at school.

I finally did get a chance to fill Kate in on my day with Zach. It was after school, and we were waiting for what promised to be an oh-so-exciting Spirit Club meeting to start. I told her all about going to the Marine Science Center and Hawaiian Rick's.

"Did Rick quiz you before he sold you the shirt?" she asked.

I laughed. "How'd you know?"

"He takes that local stuff seriously," she explained. "How much did he charge you for the shirt?"

"Two dollars."

Kate nodded. "Impressive. He must really like you."

"Which one?" I joked. "Zach or Hawaiian Rick?"

"Don't even get me started about Zach," she said. "He's head over heels."

"You really think so?"

"Were you there at lunch?"

(Even though I'd had the same feeling, it was really good to have someone else confirm it.)

"He said he wants to take me to a place called Rico's Fish Camp."

Before she could say anything, we were interrupted by a voice from behind us.

"You're going on a date with Zach Miller?"

We turned and saw that it was none other than Monica Baylor. (And here the day had been going so nicely.)

"Yes," I said.

"Not that it's any of your business," Kate added.

I don't know if it makes me a bad person, but I got a little satisfaction from the pissed-off look on her face. I knew she kind of liked Zach, and the fact that he had asked me out could not have sat well with her. Of course, she couldn't say she was pissed. She had to go all passive-aggressive on me.

"That's great," she said. "I think you two make an *interesting* couple."

I should have just let it go right there. I should have just smiled and shut up. But I have this defective gene in me that sometimes makes me continue conversations that I know are bad. I couldn't help myself.

After all, Zach had said that the two of them were friends. As much as I didn't like it, she had insight into him.

"What do you mean by 'interesting'?"

"Don't be paranoid, sweetie," she offered with total condescension. "I think Zach's great. I just worry about the two of you going to Rico's, because I'd hate for you to blow it on the first date."

This was exactly what I didn't need. But I still couldn't just shut up.

"Why? What's wrong with Rico's?"

"Nothing, if you're into scroungy, old, Florida dives," she said. "But you're Miss Hip New Yorker. I just think you'll have trouble fitting in there. That's so rude of Zach. He should think about what you like, too."

Her performance was amazing. Everything she said sounded like it was based in concern for me. But it was all designed to totally eat away at what little confidence I had.

"Don't you have a meeting to run?" Kate reminded her.

Monica smiled and went to the front of the room and gaveled the meeting to a beginning. Over the next thirty minutes the group discussed all sorts of things about the float and the upcoming work day. But all I could do was think about what Monica had said about us being "interesting" and me possibly blowing it.

She knew it too. She didn't call on me once during the meeting. Normally, she loved to call on me and try to make me seem unprepared. But this time she just let me sit there and stew, worrying more and more by the minute.

After the meeting Kate did her best to calm my nerves. She pointed out that not only was Monica jealous, but she was also in fact my mortal enemy. "A lethal combination."

"That may be true," I said. "But that doesn't mean she's wrong. I've worried all along that Zach and I have too little in common. Look at today—you almost had a heart attack because of a shirt I wore. How am I going to fit in at a place called Rico's Fish Camp?"

"Easy," she told me. "You're going to go there and be yourself. You know, the girl Zach likes. The one he constantly flirts with. The one he asked to go on a date with him. Give the guy a little credit. He picked you."

Kate made some good points and calmed me a little. But I was still in a funk that night while I was trying to do my Euro history homework. I was reading about Napoleon, and my mind wandered so much that I kept reading the same paragraph over and over.

"Hey, Darby," my dad said, leaning in through my bedroom door. "Can you come give me a hand for a moment? There's a clog in 204." He was carrying a box of tools and looked as frustrated as I felt.

"Sure," I told him. "Anything to get away from the Battle of Waterloo."

"I just need you to hold the flashlight."

I still wasn't used to seeing my father with a toolbox. He was never particularly handy back home in New York. The co-op we lived in had a super, and whenever something broke, he came and fixed it. But here there was no super. There was only Dad.

When we first moved in to the hotel, he

would call somebody to fix whatever was broken. But that quickly got expensive. So, by necessity, he started learning how to do basic repairs himself.

This was the most common one. Even though there were outdoor showers by the pool and on the boardwalk, people always forgot to rinse off the sand when they walked up from the beach. First they would track it into their rooms, and then they would clean up in the shower or sink, and the sand would clog the drain.

It had happened so often by now that Dad could fix it in about fifteen minutes—pretty impressive for a guy who'd been trading stocks and bonds on Wall Street just twelve months earlier.

"Dad," I said, as I squatted down and aimed the flashlight at the pipe he was trying to get loose. "Why did you ask Mom out? I mean the first time you asked her out."

He was lying on his back underneath the sink, so he had to twist a little to look me in the eye.

"Why do you ask that?"

"I'm just curious," I explained. "I mean,

at first glance you two don't have a lot in common. She's kind of . . . you know."

He laughed. "Yeah, I know."

"And you're the opposite. She runs marathons and listens to classical music and you like peanut-butter fudge and classic rock. What on earth made you think you'd work as a couple?"

He thought about it for a moment while he wrenched the pipe loose.

"First of all," he said, "I didn't ask her out. She asked me out."

I laughed. "Are you serious?"

"Yes," he said. "Back in college all these lumpy parts were arranged better; I was something of a catch. Your mom and I lived in the same dorm. We'd been friends all through sophomore and junior years. And then one day she told me that she didn't want to be my friend anymore. She wanted to be something more."

That sounded just like my mother. Always taking charge. "And what did you say?"

Dad wiggled the pipe free and scooted out from under the sink.

"I said what you said. I told her we

didn't have anything in common. I pointed out that we had different likes and dislikes. Different personalities. Different everything."

He stopped for a moment and smiled as he ran through the memory. "And then she said something I'll never forget."

"What did she say?"

"'So what?'"

"That's it?"

"That's it." He sat still for a moment. "'So what' changed my life forever. Two words that made me realize that two people don't need to like all the same things; they only need to like each other. And believe me, I like her a lot. I thought your mom was stunning and brilliant and funny."

I thought about it for a moment and nodded. "What happened after that?"

"Then we made out on the couch until my roommate came home."

"Dad!" I protested. "I don't want to hear about that kind of stuff."

"You were the one who asked," he said with a laugh as he dumped the sand out into a bucket. Then he slid back under the sink and started to reattach the pipe.

"Why the sudden interest in our early dating?"

"No reason," I said, completely dodging the question. "I was just curious."

I had to twist down a little to get the flashlight shining in just the right place for him to see the nut he was tightening.

"Does it have anything to do with you and Zach and Friday night?"

I was so caught off guard, I accidentally dropped the flashlight.

"I'll take that as a yes," he said.

"What makes you say that?" I asked, clearing my throat. "Why would you think anything is going on with me and Zach on Friday?" (Sometimes I wonder if my parents trained with the CIA or something. They always know way more than they should.)

"I've seen how you look at each other," he said. "And I notice that you laugh a little bit harder when he tells a joke."

I was appalled. "I do no such thing."

"Besides," he said, "he called and asked if he could have Friday off, and you got Kate to pick up your Friday shift. I was born at night, but I wasn't born last night."

Did I mention that my dad is pretty smart?

He finished tightening the pipe and scooted back out from under the sink. He sat up and looked me in the eye.

"I don't know what kind of music Zach likes. And I don't know much about surfing or whatever else he's into. But I do know one thing about him."

"What's that?" I asked.

"I know that he's smart enough to pick the right girl to ask out on a date. So he has to have something going for him."

# Eleven

Normally I would have spent the entire week obsessing about my date with Zach, but (oh, lucky me) school was able to give me plenty of other things to stress over. In one three-day period I had semester exams in physics, Spanish, and calculus, not to mention a ten-minute oral presentation in European history. (Apparently, my teachers are involved in some secret government conspiracy to make my brain explode.)

I also got dragged to my first-ever CB High basketball game by Kate. In addition to being a closet sports nut, she was also trying to get something started with the team's point guard, an exchange student from Argentina named Leandro.

"His name means 'the lion,'" she told me. "How hot is that?"

She wanted me to come along because I'm taking Spanish 4, and she thought I might be able to help in case any of her pick-up lines didn't translate properly.

I wouldn't say that I officially have Conch spirit, but the game was pretty exciting, and I got into it. It went down to the last second, and Coconut Beach was down by a point. Leandro made a great pass to a player who missed an easy layup that would have won it. As she hurried down to the court afterward, Kate turned to me and asked, "What's Spanish for 'Hey, baby, it wasn't your fault'?"

On Thursday I came home and was completely blindsided by an envelope lying on the kitchen table. I wouldn't have noticed it if it weren't for the fact that my mother was sitting there staring at it like one of those guards in front of Buckingham Palace. I looked down and instantly recognized the seal on the envelope.

It was from Columbia University.

My initial reaction was kind of like Superman's when he comes across a random chunk of kryptonite. I backed away to a careful distance and pointed at it. "When did that get here?"

"About two and a half hours ago," Mom said, her eyes still trained on it in case it made any sudden moves.

"And how long have you been staring at it like that?"

"About two and a half hours."

"Did you open it?"

"Of course not," she said. "It's addressed to you." She picked it up and handed it to me.

The first thing I noticed was its thickness. Or rather, its lack of thickness. "Thin usually means no," I said.

"Not always," Mom answered. "My first letter from Northwestern was thin." (Northwestern is where my parents went to college.)

I was surprisingly nervous. I think it was because it was the first school to send a letter. To be honest, I considered Columbia a long shot at best. It was Ivy League and in New York, so it would be great. But while my grades and test scores were up there, they weren't *up there* up there.

I flapped the envelope for a moment and then handed it to my mother. "I want you to open it."

"Why?"

I looked at her and smiled. "Because you always bring me good luck."

She momentarily broke her Buckingham Palace guard routine and smiled. "That's so sweet." She took the envelope and used a well-manicured nail to slice open one end. I could tell she was making sure that the letter stayed pristine for my scrapbook.

I took a deep breath as she started reading. Her eyes instantly turned into lasers, and her lips pulled tight against her teeth. Then she slapped the table and said the F-word.

That's how I learned I wasn't going to go to an Ivy League school. I skipped all the platitudes like "thank you for applying," "as you know, admission is extremely competitive," and "we had more worthy applications than openings." Instead I got an F-bomb from my mother. And even though I was disappointed, I couldn't help but laugh.

My mother covered her mouth, horrified at what she had just said. (She is, after all, the daughter of a Lutheran minister.)

"I am so sorry," she said.

"It's okay, Mom. I didn't expect to get into Columbia anyway."

She still looked a little stunned. "I'm sorry about that, but I can't believe I cursed in front of you. Do you think Drew heard me?"

From another room a twelve-year-old voice gleefully called out, "Yes! And it was great!"

My mom was flustered and frustrated. (Flusterated?) She began turning shades of red—a red that was part blushing because she had cussed in front of me and part anger because Columbia had dared to not accept her daughter.

In all my life I couldn't ever remember having seen her this way.

"We're getting out of here," she declared.

"To where?"

"I need junk food!" she blurted out. "How about pizza?"

"Sure," I nodded. "I love pizza."

"Can I go too?" my brother called out from his room.

"And I want to go shopping for clothes."

"Never mind," he said.

"That sounds great," I said. "Let's go."

"We'll make it a girls' day!"

Before I knew it, we were driving down A1A, and my mother was letting loose at Columbia like it was some hack trade school that had just rejected Albert Einstein.

"Do they not take into account what an incredibly well-rounded person you are?" she ranted. "And that essay you wrote for them. The one about volunteering at the summer camp for autistic children. I wept when I read that. Wept."

And that's when I started to cry. Because I hadn't known my mom had even read that essay. And I certainly hadn't known that she thought I was "incredibly well-rounded."

Of course, when I started crying, it made her start to cry. We were at a stoplight and the two of us had tears running down our cheeks.

"Columbia will rue the day," she said. (Only my mom could get away with a phrase like "rue the day.")

We were so distracted that we didn't realize the light had turned green until the car behind us honked its horn. (That was the second time in my life that I heard my mother drop an F-bomb.)

Once we wiped away all of the tears, we managed to make it to Antonio's Pizzeria, where we polished off a medium house special and a basket of garlic knots without missing a beat.

"Now we've got to find you something special to wear for your date tomorrow," she said.

"Why?" I asked. "Are you worried that Zach's going to reject me like Columbia did?"

"Yeah, right," she snorted. "Boys are actually much better than universities when it comes to picking the right girls. No, I just think you're blossoming, and blossoms deserve pretty colors."

The mention of color made me smile. "I know just the place," I said.

Mom and I attacked Hawaiian Rick's like an army invading a small island nation. We both got clothes—shirts, jeans, beach shorts, the whole deal. Rick got a kick out of my mom, and I don't think he minded staying open for an extra forty-five minutes while she made her final decisions.

I gulped when I saw the price on the cash register.

"Is that with the Coco Girl discount?" I asked.

Rick nodded. "I knocked off twenty percent."

"It's a bargain," Mom said. "We've both been wearing too much black."

"What will Dad say?" I asked.

Mom just smiled. "Nothing, unless he wants me to dump that secret stash of Cap'n Crunch."

I laughed. "You know about that?"

"Who do you think refills it every week? Did you think one box could last that long?"

The little trip turned out to be just what I needed. Not only did it help me get over the disappointment of not getting into Columbia, but it also kept me from obsessing about Zach.

Right before I went to sleep, I got a text message from Kate announcing that she had made serious progress with Leandro and would need my translation skills before school.

I crawled under my comforter and leafed through the latest copy of *Us Weekly*. (One advantage of knowing that I wasn't Ivy League–bound was that I could catch up on my celebrity gossip without feeling guilty.)

While I was lying in bed, I looked at the pictures of my New York friends flashing on my screen saver. For a while I debated back and forth whether or not I should delete the pictures of Brendan. I was about to go out with another guy, and it seemed odd to still have pictures of my old boyfriend around. Especially because to me this date wasn't just a date. Whether or not we became a couple, I knew that I was feeling something special for Zach. It was something that I had never felt for anyone but Brendan. But it was also different, maybe something more.

# Twelve

"Did I tell you how hot you look?" Kate asked. She was on her break and had run upstairs from the dining room to see me before Zach picked me up.

"I think you mentioned it," I laughed.

"Good," she reiterated. "Because you do."

I was wearing my favorite pair of low-rise skinny-leg jeans and a baby-doll tank that I'd picked up at Hawaiian Rick's. I had my hair pulled back into a ponytail, and I'd decided to go with minimal makeup. Rico's struck me as a natural setting, so I was going with *What you see is what you get.*

"By the way," Kate said. "You owe me one night's tips."

"Why?" I demanded. "Because you picked up my shift?"

"No, because we had a bet back on New Year's Day. You said I couldn't make my New Year's resolution last to the end of the month, and we're already into February. Don't you remember?"

"I remember you throwing up a lot," I told her. "What was that resolution again?"

"You know what it was!" she exclaimed. "No project boyfriends. No more losers. And I have avoided all losers for January."

"Are we sure about Leandro?"

She gave me a *how dare you* look. "Leandro is *magnifico*."

"What about my resolution?" I said. "I promised to have a better attitude, and I have done that big-time. What do I get?"

Kate gave me a look. "You get a potential boyfriend who is dreamy hot."

Just hearing that made me smile wide. "I do, don't I?"

It's funny, because even though my pet peeve is when people use two words with the same meaning, "dreamy hot" didn't bother me one bit. Well, it bothered me, but in a sweaty-palms, rapid-pulse kind of way.

I heard the elevator coming up to the third floor and took a deep breath. "You better get out of here," I told her. "I don't need you making this more odd than it already is."

Suddenly she turned into a coach sending me into a big game. "All right, but just remember: Don't talk with your mouth full. Don't put your elbows on the table. Oh, and don't be a slut."

I gave her a look. "Is that all?"

She thought about it for a second. "If you get in a situation where you don't know what to do, try to think what I would do and then do about sixty-five percent of that."

I didn't even dignify that with a response. I just pointed to the stairwell. She smiled and winked. "Did I tell you how hot you look?"

"Thanks."

She hurried down the stairs just as the elevator reached the third floor. Moments later there was a knock at the door, and my first (and potentially only) official date with Zach began.

Mom and Dad were working, and Drew was deep in a game of Guitar Hero, so I had to answer the door. I waited a moment so that I didn't seem too eager.

"Wow," he said when he saw me. "You look fantastic."

(For some reason it sounded so much better coming from him than from Kate.)

"Thanks. So do you."

Zach had a curious expression and he looked around the room.

"Are you alone?"

"Yeah—why?" I asked. "Were you expecting my brother to come along?"

"No," he laughed. "But I was expecting your father or mother to give me the whole intimidator speech about getting you back before your curfew. That's why I wore the patterned shirt. So they couldn't see me sweat."

(For some reason this struck me as extremely sweet.)

"Sorry," I told him. "Mom and Dad are both working downstairs. Besides, they kind of control your paycheck, so I think they're pretty secure in knowing that I'll be back in time."

"Excellent point!"

As we walked to the elevator, he kind of put his hand out to the side. I thought it was there for me to take, but like I've said, signals with Zach were pretty subtle.

I hesitated for a moment and then slipped my hand into his. When his fingers wrapped around mine, the fit was perfect.

I was totally gone.

"I picked out the perfect music for us," he said as we sat down in the Jeep. (By the way, he did hold my door for me.)

I ran through the obvious choices. "Iz? The White Stripes?"

He just smiled and turned on the ignition. When the radio turned on, the reception was a little scratchy, and the music was all in Spanish. It took a moment, but then it hit me.

"The station we were listening to in the truck?" I said.

*"El gigante ocho setenta,"* he said with a cheesy Spanish accent. *"Todas las clásicas, todo el tiempo."*

"Is that what it's really called?"

He nodded and laughed. "I tracked down their website. They broadcast out of Miami."

I was amazed at how relaxed I felt. I had expected to be a bundle of nerves. Zach, on the other hand, looked like he was going to pass out.

We drove south on A1A, and I noticed something seemed different about the Jeep. Then it hit me. He had cleaned and waxed it. The interior had been scrubbed, and the seat even felt a little slippery.

"Tell me about this place we're going for dinner."

"Rico's is down on the Intracoastal," he said. (The Intracoastal Waterway runs parallel to the ocean all along the East Coast.) "It's been there forever, and every Friday they have a fish fry that is out of this world."

Rico's is a concrete box of a building next to a marina. The paint is peeling in parts, and the right half of the neon sign is burned out, so it reads RI FI CA.

To be honest, a few New York Darby instincts kicked in, and I almost suggested going somewhere else. Monica had said I wouldn't fit in, and she may have been right on target. I could tell that Zach was worried about my reaction.

"I know it doesn't look like much," he said, "but trust me. You're going to love it."

So far he'd been right about the Marine Science Center and about Hawaiian Rick's. The least I could do was trust him. Still, the best I could come up with was, "If you say so."

The inside was no better than the out. Nothing matched. The tables and chairs were all shapes and sizes and looked like they came from garage sales. The place was packed, but there was no food on any of the tables. The people were just sitting there.

We were greeted at the door by an older woman who obviously went a different direction with regard to the natural look: She wore enough makeup for two, and her waitress uniform looked like it fit her snugly twenty-five pounds ago.

"Hi, Zach," she said the moment she saw him. "Who's this?"

"Lucille, I want you to meet Darby. Darby, this is Lucille."

Lucille gave me a big smile, and I tried not to stare at the lipstick smear on her teeth. "Nice to meet you, Darby."

"Nice to meet you," I said.

Lucille led us to a small table by the far wall. The table wobbled when I put my hand on it.

"What can I get you to drink?" she asked us.

I couldn't imagine drinking the water. "I'll take a Coke." (I resisted the urge to add, *in a can, please*.)

"Coke for me, too," Zach said.

I waited for Lucille to hand us a menu. But then I realized she wasn't carrying any. There weren't any on the table, either.

"Menu?" I asked Zach.

"They don't really have menus," he said. "We pretty much eat whatever Rico feels like making."

A few minutes later Rico came out from the kitchen. He was tall and thin and looked to be in his fifties. He had a bushy mustache and wavy gray hair and carried a handbell.

He started ringing the bell and chanted, "Hot shrimp! Get 'em while they're hot, hot, hot!"

As he said it, everyone in the room (except for me) chanted "hot, hot, hot" right along with him. Lucille led a group of serv-ers out of the kitchen, and each of them was carrying a platter overflowing with fried shrimp.

They quickly went from table to table, giving the people as much as they wanted. Lucille came to our table and put a scoopful on my plate. Then she stood there and stared.

"What's wrong?" I asked her.

She smiled. "I want to see you try one."

I felt more than a little self-conscious, but I realized she wasn't going to leave until I ate one. I took a bite and couldn't believe it. It was one of the most delicious things I had ever eaten.

"There it is," she said with a laugh.

"There what is?" I asked.

"I call it the shrimp moment," Lucille explained. "Because shrimp is always what we serve first. It's that moment you realize something you were worried about might just be great."

The rest of the meal continued the same way. Every ten minutes or so Rico would come out and ring the bell and announce the next course. Then everyone (including me) would join in and chant, "Eat it while it's hot, hot, hot!"

After the meal another chant broke out, and this time I didn't hesitate to join in.

"Cookie Monster! Cookie Monster!"

Rico came out with a cookie sheet in one hand and a spatula in the other. He went around from table to table and flipped off cookies onto people's plates. When a tray was done, he'd put it down on the table, and Lucille would hand him another one.

Because we were against the wall, we were the last table. Rico smiled at me.

"Did you enjoy your dinner?" he asked.

"Yes," I told him. "Very much."

He flipped a couple of cookies into the air and they plopped down on my plate. Then he did the same for Zach.

Like everything else about the meal, the cookies were off-the-chart delicious.

After dinner we walked barefoot along the beach, right along the waterline.

"I've always wondered," Zach said. "What brought you guys to Coconut Beach?"

I laughed. "That's a good question. I'm not even sure I know the whole answer. My dad worked on Wall Street, and I thought he was happy, but I guess he wasn't. One day he decided that he just couldn't take it anymore and wanted to quit."

"But how'd he pick the Seabreeze?"

"He grew up in Michigan, and every year his family would drive down to Florida for vacation. They'd always spend a week at the Seabreeze. He just loved it and always wanted to come back."

"What about you?" he said. "What do you think of our little beach town?"

I thought for a moment, trying to come up with just the right words. "It's growing on me," I said. "But it helps that I have an expert spirit guide leading the way."

He stopped and made a circle in the sand. "Shark's tooth."

I looked down, and the moonlight fully illuminated the shells at our feet. I looked hard, and this time I actually found the shark's tooth.

"Nice," he said as I picked it up and slipped it into my front pocket.

Our walk ended at the Tenth Street Pier, which stretched out about a hundred feet into the ocean. People liked to fish off it, and at the end there was a spot with no railing and a ladder down to the water. We sat there and let our feet dangle over the edge.

Zach put his arm around me and pulled me close to him. Then he gave me the best kiss I had ever gotten. It was wet and messy and incredibly romantic. Everything about it was perfect, and I was in love.

That's why I would never have guessed that within twenty-four hours we wouldn't even be talking to each other.

# Thirteen

With the exception of getting rejected by Columbia, my life actually seemed to be working out. That alone should have been a clue that trouble was brewing, but I was too drunk on romance and love to notice.

When I woke up Saturday morning, I walked out onto the balcony and couldn't believe how beautiful the beach looked. And since I knew there had been no major earthquakes or hurricanes to alter its appearance, I realized the change was not in the beach, but in the way that I looked at it.

This transformation was not just because of my wicked crush on Zach (although that was certainly a big part of it). It was also because of a huge Hawaiian man who sold you shirts based on how much he liked you and grown-ups who chanted for cookies like a pack of preschoolers and little kids who searched the sand for sharks' teeth. I used to call Coconut Beach godforsaken. But now I realized that it was actually quite special.

This burst of civic pride could not have come at a better time, because this was the day we were meeting to build our float in the hotel parking lot. Originally I'd only gotten involved to tweak Monica, but now I was actually looking forward to the parade.

Kate arrived a half hour early so that she could grill me about my date with Zach.

"Tell me all the horny details!" she blurted out the second I opened the door. I shushed her and nodded to my parents in the next room. We went out onto the balcony for privacy.

The second the sliding glass door shut, she started. "How did it go? How did it go?"

I didn't even answer. I just looked at her and flashed a big old goober smile.

"That good?" She grinned. "That's excellent."

I nodded and proceeded to fill her in on the highlights from Rico's Fish Camp, our walk down the beach, and the kiss on the pier. I made sure to include a lot of adjectives like "passionate," "dazzling," and the ever-popular "toe-curling."

She was especially pleased by the last bit of info.

"That's big," she said with great satisfaction. "Once you've been kissed on the end of the Tenth Street Pier, you are a full-on Coco Girl."

I took a deep breath of the cool, salty air. "I guess I am."

"And the best part," Kate said, "is that you don't have to pace around your room and get in that New York funk of yours worrying about whether or not he's going to call you or if you should text him, because he should be arriving here in about fifteen minutes for the work day."

"How perfect is that?" I said. "Let's give it up for the Spirit Club parade float."

"You're welcome, by the way," she said. "You know, I kind of masterminded that whole thing."

"Is that so?"

"I'm an evil genius of sorts," she joked. "I may even go to Kinko's and get me some business cards."

She was joking, but she was also right. I was lucky to have a friend like Kate looking out for me and encouraging me when I began to have doubts.

"Thanks, Kate."

"My pleasure."

The float turned out to be a much bigger project than I ever would have guessed. Luckily, since the whole town gets involved in the parade, the hardware store had already ordered a lot of supplies.

Our "musical conch" was being built on a flatbed trailer that one of the girls got from her father's lawn-care business. There were about a dozen Spirit Club members working on it, along with a handful of extra helpers like Zach.

It was great to see him, but also a little awkward, because there were so many people around. When he got there, I didn't know if I should go over and kiss him or if I should just play it cool. (I ended up opting for cool, which in this instance is just another word for chicken.)

"Thanks for helping," I said with that same goober smile plastered on my face as I worked my eye-flirt magic.

"My pleasure," he said. "But don't forget our deal, surfer girl."

"Don't worry," I said with a pretend shiver. "I won't."

We broke up into two groups. One was responsible for decorating the trailer and covering it with a colorful plastic material called floral sheeting. The other tried to make the giant conch out of chicken wire. I was in the conch group along with Kate, Zach (hooray), and Monica.

Bending the chicken wire and getting it to hold shape took a lot of muscle and patience.

"This is pretty difficult," I said as Kate and I tried to bend one portion.

"You're telling me," Kate answered, her voice straining.

"I tried to warn everybody," Monica said to Zach. "The giant conch is just a bad idea."

(At this point I momentarily fantasized about wrapping the chicken wire around her.)

"I think it's a great idea," Zach said. "It's definitely going to be the best float in the whole parade." (Darby 1, Monica 0)

Not only was Zach friendly and nice to look at, but he was essential in building the float. Shaping surfboards had given him a good feel for construction, and working at the Marine Science Center meant he could help us make the conch look like an actual shell instead of a blob.

"That is looking great," my mother said as she came out from the hotel to check on us. She brought a cooler with some drinks for a break.

By that point the base had been completed and was all glittery. The chicken-wire structure of the conch was in place, and now we were decorating it.

"It's getting there," Kate said.

"Absolutely," added Zach.

(I knew they were right, because rather than deliver one of her snarky little comments, Monica just kept her mouth shut.)

For music I plugged some speakers into my iPod and turned it on full blast. I had downloaded five different versions of the song "Sea of Love." Even though the lyrics were all the same, the music sounded different, as each artist gave the song a different spin and feel. There was the original by Phil Phillips, an alt version by Cat Power, one that sounded kind of folk/country, and another one that was reggae. The fifth one, though, was my favorite. I watched Zach to see his reaction when he heard it.

About ten seconds into it he stopped what he was doing and looked right at me. "Wait a second, is that Iz? I didn't know he sang a cover of this song."

"What?" I asked in my best mocking tone. "There's something about Israel Kamakawiwoʻole that you don't know? And you call yourself a fan. I'm going to have to go tell Hawaiian Rick. He will not be pleased."

Zach laughed, and Kate started to do a little hula along with the music. It was hilarious how she tried to act out the lyrics with her hands and sing along. Most of the others sang along too. (Well, everybody but Monica.)

I was stapling letters that spelled out THIS IS CONCH COUNTRY along one side of the float when I noticed a jet-black Porsche with tinted windows pull into the parking lot. It only caught my attention because it was so out of place. The Seabreeze parking lot is normally the land of SUVs, minivans, and station wagons; we don't get a lot of fancy sports cars. But I didn't pay much attention to it and squatted back down to keep stapling on the letters.

From my vantage point I could only see the lower half of the car as it pulled into the spot next to the float and parked. When the car door opened and the driver got out, I could only see his shoes. He was wearing a pair of black leather Bruno Magli loafers—also something you don't see very often at the Seabreeze.

"Can I help you?" somebody asked.

"I'm looking for a girl named Darby McCray."

I recognized the voice in an instant. It was like a bad dream that I couldn't make myself wake up from.

"Is Darby a friend of yours?" Kate asked.

"A lot more than that," he said. "She's my girlfriend."

I stood up slowly and saw Brendan

standing right there next to the Porsche. When he saw me, he flashed his perfect smile.

"It's great to see you, D.," he said.

"Brendan," I stuttered as I fought with the throb developing in my forehead. "What are you doing here? In Florida?"

He shook his head playfully, and I got the distinct impression that this was as much for everyone else as it was for me. "I travel twelve hundred miles to see my girl, and that's the welcome I get?"

My mind went totally blank. I was too shocked to say anything. I looked over at Zach, who had the saddest, most confused expression I had ever seen. I could tell he wanted me to give him an explanation, but I couldn't.

Brendan, of course, was oblivious to all of this. He specialized in grand gestures and flashy entrances. I'm sure he thought this was his best ever.

He walked around the float toward me, and he answered my question but did it as though he were talking to everyone. "My father is in Palm Beach for a golf weekend with Donald Trump." (As he did with all name-dropping, he said "Donald Trump" as a little sideways whisper.) "They flew down on the private jet, of course, and there was extra room. So I came along so that I could come over here and rescue you from all of this."

He reached me right when he got to "rescue you," and when he did, he looked around at all of the tools and materials and added, "And not a moment too soon, I can see."

I was horrified. So horrified that I still couldn't say or do anything. (How is it possible that I had never realized how pompous Brendan was?)

Then to finish his little monologue, he threw his arms around me and gave me a huge kiss.

It was the worst moment of my life.

"Come on, baby," he said, motioning to the Porsche. "Let's go have some fun."

I was finally able to form words, and I decide to hold my ground. "I can't go anywhere," I told him. "We're not done."

Now it was Brendan who had the stunned look. Although he tried to play it off as a joke. "You can't be serious. I just traveled over a thousand miles to visit you, and you're too busy?"

"You could have called or e-mailed or something to let me know," I explained. "I didn't know you were coming, and I promised I'd help with the float. I can't leave until it's done."

"Don't be ridiculous." I looked up and saw that it was Monica talking. "We've got this covered. You go on and go, girl."

*She did not just "go on and go, girl" me. Un-freaking-believable.*

I tried to make eye contact with Zach, but he was not looking my way. I couldn't tell if he was angry or sad.

"You see," Brendan said, taking Monica's lead. "They want you to go too. This is incredibly romantic stuff here."

He turned to them. "Don't you think she should go with me?"

There was a moment of quiet, and even Monica didn't answer. Finally, one voice did.

"Yes," Zach said. "She should go with you."

# Fourteen

"How could you do that?" I demanded as we pulled out of the parking lot.

"What are you talking about?" Brendan exclaimed.

I pointed back toward the hotel. "That show you just put on. I've never been so embarrassed in my life. Those are my friends."

Brendan couldn't believe it. "Friends? Aren't you the one who wrote me an e-mail about how she hated everyone and everything down here?"

That was in fact true, but I was in no mood to be reminded of it. All I could think about was Zach and what he must be thinking about me.

"I wrote that e-mail a long time ago," I reminded him. "Things have gotten better. A lot better."

"Good for you," Brendan said. "I still don't see the problem. I thought that was pretty romantic."

"There you go! *That* is the problem," I explained. "Where do you get off playing the 'look how romantic I am' card? And where do you get off telling everyone that I'm your girlfriend?"

This caught his attention, and he pulled the car off the road into a strip-mall parking lot. He took a deep breath and turned to me. "You're not my girlfriend?"

"Not that I'm aware of," I replied. I had recovered from my initial stunned reaction and was now back on my A-game. "I got some sweet 'hey baby' phone calls when I first moved down here, but you've sent me what, five e-mails since Thanksgiving? Oh, and a family Christmas card signed by your *mother*."

(I had some theories as to why things had played out the way they had. Like I said, Brendan and I had never officially broken up, but we also hadn't said anything about keeping things going long-distance. There'd been some talk about me coming up to New York at Christmas, but that had mysteriously disappeared in the middle of November, and I assumed Brendan had found a new girl. My guess now was that they had just broken up.)

"My bad," he said.

That almost did it. "You did not just say 'my bad' like you took a bad shot playing basketball with your friends."

"I didn't mean it that way," he said. "It was bad of me. It was totally lame. But you know I'm not good at long distance."

"Well, then we've got a problem," I explained, "because we live twelve hundred miles apart. That's pretty long-distance."

He smiled. "But not for long."

This caught me off guard. "What do you mean?"

"Next year you'll be back in New York for college, and I'll be a senior at Hendricks-Hudson." (Hendricks-Hudson was the name of Brendan's prep school. He was a year behind me in school.)

"Things will go back to normal," he

continued. "You and me in NYC. Things the way they're supposed to be."

The fact that the line rhymed and sounded eerily like a bad song lyric made me think he had spent some time practicing it. But the reality was that I probably would be in New York next year. Columbia was out of the running, but I was still expecting to wind up at Vassar, Sarah Lawrence, or NYU. Come fall, Brendan would be right around the corner, and Zach was hoping to be in California.

"Where are you even taking me?" I asked him.

Brendan kind of shrugged. "I don't know," he said. "I just wanted to come and sweep you off your feet."

I shook my head.

"Well, you really suck at this," I told him. "You rescue a damsel in distress who isn't in distress and then you throw her on your trusty steed and have no idea where you're taking her."

"That's why I need you," he said sheepishly. "You're always good at those details. I've really missed you, Darby."

For the first time, he looked a little

vulnerable and as a result was kind of cute. I had missed him, too.

"I thought maybe we could get some lunch and talk," he said. "But I don't know any good places around here."

The shock had worn off, and I tried to figure out what I should do. Had this been a few weeks earlier, I would have thought it was all incredibly romantic. But that was before Zach and I became a couple. Now I really didn't know what I felt. But I was pretty sure I couldn't go back to the Seabreeze and do any damage control. That was definitely a hot zone.

"I know some good places," I said. "How about some pizza?"

Brendan smiled. "They have pizza down here?"

"Yes," I answered.

"Do they have Italians?"

"Just a few to run the pizza shops." I shook my head and wondered if this was how I had acted when I arrived from New York.

We went to Antonio's, the same place I had gone with my mother after the Columbia rejection debacle. For a second I worried that I saw some of the parade crew there, but it was just my rampant paranoia.

After we ordered a medium pepperoni pizza, I excused myself to the restroom and sent Kate an emergency text: NO TIME TO EXPLAIN BUT IT'S NOT WHAT YOU THINK. PLEASE HELP! KEEP THINGS UNDER CONTROL.

I put the phone down next to the sink and splashed some water on my face. A few seconds later, the phone started to vibrate across the tile. I picked it up and read Kate's two-word response: TOO LATE.

The night before, I'd been sitting with Zach on the end of the Tenth Street Pier, having the most romantic moment in my life. And now I didn't even know what to think.

When I went back to the table, Brendan looked a little nervous. "What's the matter?" I asked him.

"The people," he said. "They keep saying hello and acting like they know me."

"Don't worry," I laughed. "They do that down here. It took me a while to get used to it too."

He looked at me for a moment, unsure what to say. I decided to take a chance.

"When did you two break up?" I asked.

He looked a little surprised and tried to play it cool. "What two?"

"You and the girl you started dating back in November."

He knew better than to lie to me. "Did somebody tell you about her?"

"No. I just figured it out." (I left off the part about him being so incredibly transparent.)

"Her name is Rebecca," he said. "We broke up about two weeks ago."

(How weird is this? I'd assumed that he was dating. *I* was dating. But for some reason just hearing the name Rebecca made her real and made me jealous. It's totally baffling.)

I gave him my all-knowing look. "And now you're heartbroken, so you come down here to sweep me off my feet."

"I broke it off with her," he said. "That's the truth. And it made me realize how much I missed you. When my dad asked me if I wanted to come down to Florida with him, the first thing I thought of was surprising you."

"I guess that's a little sweet," I said.

"I also wanted to give you this." He reached into his pocket and pulled out an envelope.

"What is it?"

"It's a voucher for a plane ticket," he said. "It's from my dad's frequent-flyer miles. You can cash it in for one round-trip ticket to New York."

"I do miss New York," I admitted.

He reached across the table and held my hand. "I was hoping you could use it to come up next weekend."

"Why next weekend?"

"Hadley Montgomery is having her big Valentine's bash. She's dying for you to come. I thought we could go together. Just like old times." He gave me a long, hard look. "And maybe just like new times."

Now my head was completely spinning. "What do you mean by that?"

"You could come up for Valentine's," he explained. "And maybe I could come down for part of Spring Break and stay at the hotel. Then we could see each other over the summer a couple times, and when you come back to school in the fall, we could be a full-time couple again."

"Wow," I said. "You've really thought this thing through."

He nodded. "Everything except for the part when I drove up in the Porsche and found you with all of those other people. That part I hadn't thought through."

"Yeah, I kind of got that," I said.

It turned out he had to drive back to Palm Beach that night, so after we had our pizza, I showed him around town. It was weird, because normally other people were showing me around town, and now I was the one talking about how cool it was and how interesting things were. We stopped by Hawaiian Rick's, but I don't think Rick liked him much, because he charged him full price on a T-shirt.

The whole thing was kind of surreal. Every now and then I'd think about Zach and wonder how he was reacting to all of this. Every ten minutes or so I'd check my messages to see if he had sent a text, but my mailbox was always empty.

Before Brendan had to leave, I took him down to the beach for a walk. When we reached the sand, I looked down and laughed.

"I can't believe you're wearing those shoes."

"My favorite pair of Bruno Maglis?"

"How much did they cost?"

He shrugged. "I don't know. About three hundred and fifty bucks."

A year ago that might have impressed me, but now it just seemed like a total waste.

"Well, you better not wear them on the beach," I warned him. "They'll probably get ruined."

He took them off and carried them in his hand. We walked close to each other, but we didn't touch or hold hands. It was awkward. Extremely awkward. I felt like a total slut because part of me still liked Brendan. And another part seriously thought about using the ticket to go up to New York and party at Hadley's place on the Upper East Side.

Brendan, though, was a wreck on the beach. He kept walking like the shells were hurting the bottoms of his feet. And when, amazingly, I found a shark's tooth with absolutely no help from anybody, he was less than impressed.

We ended up at the Tenth Street Pier.

All I could think of was how Kate had warned me that she sees everything. I could just imagine her spying on me, thinking I was the biggest slut at CB High.

"What's that smell?" Brendan asked, his nose at full crinkle. "Bait?"

"Probably," I said.

He hacked a couple of times, and I had to fight the urge to laugh. (Surprisingly, I hadn't noticed any smell the night before when I'd been there with Zach.)

We walked down to the end of the pier and sat down in the same spot where Zach and I had kissed. Actually, I sat down, and Brendan hemmed and hawed for a moment, worried that the dampness of the pier might ruin his shorts.

"They're Ralph Lauren," he said. "Brand-new."

I took off my hoodie and laid it down for him to sit on.

"Thanks," he said.

We just looked out at the waves for a moment. I wondered if what he had predicted could come true. Was it possible for us to get back together and be a couple when I went to college?

"I love you, Darby," he said. And he leaned over and gave me a big kiss. I didn't fight it, but I also didn't welcome it. I didn't know what to think. And I didn't know what the future held.

But I did know one thing.

Not a single muscle in my toes so much as twitched.

# Fifteen

The moment Brendan left for Palm Beach I rushed into my room and tried to reach Zach. I wasn't sure if he'd take my call, but I wanted to explain everything. In Kate's text she had said it was "too late," but I thought I still might be able to fix things. He didn't answer his cell phone, so I tried his house. His mom answered.

"Hi, Mrs. Miller, this is Darby," I told her, wondering if she had already branded me a two-timing woman. "Is Zach there?"

"I haven't seen him since this afternoon," she said. "I'm not sure where he went."

I tried to read the tone of her voice, but there was no way to know if she was telling the truth or not. For all I knew, Zach was just sitting there signaling her to say no.

"Do you want me to give him a message?"

I thought about it for a moment. "Just tell him I really want to talk to him, please . . . and tell him I'm sorry."

"Sure thing, Darby."

My next step was to track Kate down. I got her on her cell.

"Where are you?" I asked her. "I need to talk!"

"I'm kind of busy right now," she said. "Remember my date with Leandro?"

(What a crappy friend I am. I get so focused on my train wreck of a life that I forget my friends have lives too.)

"I'm sorry," I said. "I'll let you go. But . . . do you have any idea where Zach is?"

There was a pause on the other end of the line. "Somewhere with Monica . . . sorry."

"There's nothing for you to be sorry about," I said. "This is all on me. Have fun on your date. I'll want to hear all about it."

It had been my worry all day that

Monica would make her move. She'd been right there when Brendan arrived and turned everything upside down. I was sure she'd seen her chance with Zach and gone for it on the spot.

For a little while I actually considered going out and looking for them and forcing the issue. (Not one of my best ideas.) But luckily, I realized that there had already been way too much drama for one day. Instead I went out to my secret spot on the roof.

I looked out at the ocean and thought about everything. I thought about Zach and how he made me feel. And I thought about Brendan and the plane ticket. I tried to imagine what it would be like when I was in college.

I heard something and turned to see my mother climbing over my balcony with a folding beach chair in one hand.

"I know this is your secret spot," she said. "But I was worried about you."

"Jeez," I said. "First the stash of Cap'n Crunch and now my special spot. Do you know all my secrets?"

"I'm your mother," she said. "I've trained my whole life for this."

I smiled at her, but she could tell that I was hurting. She came over and put her chair right next to mine.

"Talk to me," she said. "I'm sure we can figure it out."

I sat there for a moment, unsure where to start. Then I told her everything. I walked her through all the key moments with Zach and how he made me feel. I told her that I thought I was in love with him.

I expected her to jump in and say I was too young to be in love or something like that, but she didn't even flinch.

I talked about Brendan and his plan for next year when I'd be in college, and all about the plane ticket and Hadley's party. I even told her that Monica was my evil nemesis and had apparently already swooped in on Zach.

She listened to all of it without saying a word. Her only expression was of total concern. When I was done, she pulled a Kleenex out of her pocket and handed it to me. She waited a moment to make sure I didn't have anything else to say.

Finally, she started to talk. "First of all," she said, "you didn't do a single thing wrong.

It's important for you to know that."

"Did you listen to any of what I just said?" I pleaded. "I did everything wrong."

"You liked a boy, and he liked you back. That's not wrong. Then another boy who also liked you arrived uninvited. That was beyond your control. You were polite. You were proper. And you were honest. So, no, you didn't do anything wrong."

When she said that, it made me feel much better. My mother is very moral. (Remember, she's a minister's kid.) If she says I'm on firm ground, then it's probably true. I took a deep breath and nodded for her to keep going.

"It's true that you might get back together with Brendan next year, but I think it's also true that you don't feel for him the same way that you feel for Zach."

"You're right."

"I'm not going to tell you that you can't go to New York for the party. I know you miss your friends. I know you miss the city. But you need to really ask yourself, is it fair to Brendan? What message would you be sending him if you went up there?"

I hadn't really thought much about Brendan's feelings in that regard. It would be totally leading him on for me to fly in on Valentine's Day for a romantic weekend.

"Then what should I do?"

"I can't tell you what to do," she said. "I can only tell you what I would do if it were me."

I looked at her hopefully. Maybe she had some brilliant solution that had thus far eluded me.

"Am I going to like it?"

She laughed. "Probably not."

"Tell me anyway."

"I would stay here and go to all the Valentine's Day celebrations. I would go to the Big Swim and the parade and the picnic and Cupid's Ball."

"I'm worried that Zach is going to be there with Monica," I pointed out. "And I would be there all alone."

She looked at me and smiled.

"So what?"

I waited for more, but that was it. She stood up, folded her chair, and gave me a kiss before heading back into the house through my window. It was the same line that my father said had changed his life when they started dating. But I wasn't sure it would work out as well for me.

Going alone would really suck.

The next day Hadley Montgomery called and gave me the hard sell for the party. She said it was going to be epic and that Brendan was dying for me to come back to New York. Her dad was arranging for a great band, and of course there would be the cranium-sized shrimp.

This sounded like the opposite of sucking.

But Mom was right. Going to New York wouldn't be fair to Brendan. And ultimately, it wouldn't be fair to me. I told Hadley I couldn't make it. Then I called Brendan, thanked him for the ticket, and told him I would mail it back to him.

It was a decision I doubted more than once during the period I affectionately named the Week from Hell.

I did get a chance to talk to Zach before school on Monday. I caught up with him by his locker.

"I really want to explain what happened," I said.

He looked at me and shook his head. "Do you have any idea what that was like for me?"

"I know, it's just . . ." I tried to come up with the right words. "Really complicated."

He shook his head. "It's not complicated at all. I trusted you, and that was a mistake."

He shut his locker and stormed off in the other direction. (Like I said, it was the Week from Hell.)

Being without a boyfriend around Valentine's Day is bad enough. Being without one in Coconut Beach was almost unbearable. There were decorations hanging in the window of every store and banners hanging over the street. (Beach Avenue was even officially renamed Lovers' Lane for the week.) Everywhere I looked, there were flowers and hearts and little baby cupids shooting their arrows. And every time I tried to talk to Zach, there was Monica looming by and clutching him on the arm.

Kate was awesome. (Without her I might have lost it.) She cheered me up every day at lunch and even tried to set me up with one of Leandro's teammates.

"He's cute," I told her. "But I only want to go with Zach."

She waved her hand in front of my face to make sure I hadn't gone crazy. "You do know that Zach is going with someone else?"

I nodded. "Yeah. I think I heard something about that."

"Did I ever tell you how smooth you are?"

We both just laughed.

One day after school I went to Hawaiian Rick's. As always, Iz was playing over the stereo, and Rick had a huge smile on his face.

"Hello, brand-new Coco Girl," he said in his booming voice. "What brings you down here alone?"

"I'm on a mission," I told him. "I want to learn how to surf, but I'm on a limited budget."

I handed him all of the tip money I had saved for the last few months. He looked at it and thought for a moment.

"I think we can make this work."

We spent the next hour digging around

the shop. He found me a used board. "Fat and thick," he said. "You gotta start on a board that is fat and thick."

We picked out a leash to connect the board to my ankle and a bar of something called Mr. Zogs Sex Wax.

"Don't worry," he told me. "It's not what you think."

"Good," I said with a laugh.

Finally, he helped me pick out a wet suit. He had me try on a couple to make sure one fit just right.

"It'll keep you warm, no matter how cold the water is," he explained. "But you can't wear it tomorrow during the Big Swim."

"I know," I told him. "If you want to earn a T-shirt, you can only wear a bathing suit."

"You got that right."

Amazingly, the total was exactly the same as the tip money that I had given him. If we were in New York, I'd assume that I was getting ripped off. But with Rick I was certain he was the one getting the short end of the deal.

"You got someone to teach you?" he asked.

I shook my head. "Not at the moment."

He thought about this. "You're a prime *wahine*," he said. "If you can't find somebody, I'll teach you."

"Okay," I said. "I just may take you up on that."

"You do that, Coco Girl." He flashed his big smile and let loose with a booming laugh. "One more thing before you go."

He reached down below the counter and pulled out a bumper sticker and handed it to me. It read EDDIE WOULD GO.

"What's this?" I asked him.

"I told you about my wall of legends," he said, indicating the wall behind him.

I nodded.

"This one is Eddie Aikau." He pointed to one of the pictures.

"He's the lifeguard, right?"

He smiled. "You do listen. He was a great surfer and the greatest lifeguard ever. He never lost a single person, which is saying a lot on the North Shore. Whenever the waves were too rough and the other lifeguards were too scared to go out . . ."

"Eddie would go," I said.

He nodded. "That's right. And whenever

I face something difficult, I remind myself of Eddie's bravery and try to be brave too."

I took the bumper sticker and smiled. "Thank you."

"I don't give those to just anyone," he said.

I nodded and knew that it was true.

The night before Valentine's Day the dining room was closed; all of the staff were busy decorating for Cupid's Ball. To call it awkward would be an understatement. (Awkward was when Uncle Gene brought a date to his wife's funeral. This was worse than that.)

Kate was working the helium machine, blowing up pink and red balloons (and making her voice sound like a Munchkin), while I was on top of a ladder trying to hang streamers from the ceiling. Zach was there arranging tables, and Monica was practically glued to his hip putting out centerpieces.

It was weird, because a couple of times I got the impression that Zach wanted to talk, but we just didn't get the chance. (Monica is dogged in her determination.)

Finally, my mother came to the rescue and told Monica that she needed her help unloading some chairs. Monica obviously didn't want to leave Zach alone, but she didn't have much of a choice. As they walked out of the room, my mother winked at me. (You gotta love Mom.)

"Here, let me help you with that," Zach said, moving a ladder over near mine. I was trying to hang a banner at the time, and it wasn't going very well.

"Thanks," I said, surprised that he had initiated the conversation.

He took one end of the banner and climbed to the top of his ladder. For a moment the two of us were up above everyone else. He looked at me and smiled. "I heard you stopped by Rick's and got some gear."

I nodded. "I hear that surfing is a lot of fun."

We both smiled, and for a brief moment it felt like things were all right again. Then I heard Monica pushing a cart of chairs back into the room, and I knew that that feeling was about to go away.

"I'm sorry," I said.

He looked at me for a second. "So am I."

I didn't get another chance to talk to him, and I had so much to say. Instead I wrote him a note and slipped it into his backpack. I couldn't be sure that he would get it, but it was the only place I could maybe get it to him without Monica seeing.

The note said:

Dear Zach,
I am so sorry for how things have turned out. I want you to know that despite what he said, Brendan has not been my boyfriend for quite a long time. I would never have lied to you about that. I can't thank you enough for being such a good friend and a wonderful spirit guide. You have helped me fall in love with my new home. And for that I will always be indebted to you. One day, if you're still willing, I would love to take you up on your offer to teach me how to surf.
Happy Valentine's Day,
Darby

P.S. I love you.

Before I sealed the envelope, I slid in the shark's tooth that I had found on my own.

# Sixteen

For breakfast on Valentine's Day my entire family ate Cap'n Crunch cereal. (Yes, even Mom.) She didn't admit to knowing about our secret stash; instead she came up with a story about how she saw a box in the store and remembered that we used to like it when we were little. (I knew she knew. And she knew that I knew she knew. But my father and brother were completely clueless.)

"Cap'n Crunch," my father said, trying to sound disinterested. "I didn't even know they still made that."

My mother and I just shared a look and shook our heads.

Dad also had a surprise for us. Since the day was filled with different competitions, he thought everybody should know who we were. He handed out pink T-shirts with TEAM MCCRAY written across the chest.

Mom and I were an easy sell, but Drew was having none of it. "No way am I wearing a pink T-shirt," he said.

My dad looked at him and nodded as if to say, *I can respect that.* Then Dad went over and picked up a box. He opened it and pulled out a set of wings, a bow and arrow, and a little sheet.

"What's that?" my brother asked nervously.

"That's the baby cupid costume for tonight's party," he said. "The one you're going to wear if you don't put on the T-shirt."

Drew thought for a moment, and a panicked look came over him. Our dad just might think that was a funny thing to do to his kid. Drew weighed his options for a moment and quickly slipped on the T-shirt. "Kind of roomy," he said, stretching his arms around. "I like it."

Clad in pink, we all headed down to

the boardwalk to begin the festivities. It seemed like everyone who lives in Coconut Beach was down there milling around. Kate and her mom stood with my family, but I couldn't find Zach in the crowd. The mayor stood up on a bench with a bullhorn.

"Happy Valentine's Day!"

"Happy Valentine's Day!" the crowd shouted back.

"Are you ready for the Big Swim?"

There were raucous cheers. I looked over at my mother, and we both laughed at the spectacle of the whole thing.

"With no further ado, let me turn things over to the big *kahuna* of the Big Swim—our very own Hawaiian Rick Keliikipi!"

Now the party was really starting up, because the people began clapping in rhythm as Rick moved to the front of the crowd. As he walked, he did some funky hula moves with his hands, juicing the crowd even more.

Rick didn't have to stand up on the bench to be seen. And he didn't need a bullhorn to be heard.

"Aloooohhhaaa!" he shouted out with amazing volume.

"Aloooohhhaaa!" everyone shouted back.

He held up a red long-sleeved T-shirt with a really cool silk-screen design on the front. On the back it had block letters that read I SWIM BIG.

"I designed this shirt myself," he said. "And the only way to get one is to go in the water and go all the way under."

The crowd cheered some more.

"But you've got to remember the rules," he called out. "What's rule number one?"

"No wet suits!" people answered.

"That's right," he said with a big toothy grin. "Bathing suits only. And what's rule number two?"

"No whining!"

"You got that right," he said. Then Rick started to strip off his shirt to reveal a rather ample stomach and a chest and back covered with tattoos. There were whistles and cheers, and he did some more hula moves. It was hilarious.

"Now, who's with me?"

Not a lot of people moved at first. It was cold outside, and the water had to be freezing. Zach and a few of the surf boys stepped forward to join him. They stripped off their shirts too, only they didn't have quite the insulation Rick had. I could see goose bumps all across Zach's body. (Okay, yes, I was checking out his body.)

A voice near me called out, "I'm in." I turned and was surprised to see my dad step out in front of the crowd. He pulled off his pink TEAM McCRAY shirt to reveal the whitest chest I had ever seen. There was a lot of laughter (especially from my mother), and Kate put her fingers in her mouth and blew an incredibly loud whistle. Dad played up to the crowd, posing and flexing like a bodybuilder. He even grabbed hold of his stomach and made it bounce around like a bowl of Jell-O. (That's when my mother covered her face in shame.)

Then another voice called out, "I'm in too." Much to my amazement, it belonged to me. My voice didn't carry as well as the others, but the moment I stepped in front of the crowd, a roar erupted.

"Check out my primo *wahine*!" Hawaiian Rick shouted as the crowd began to go crazy. He turned to me. "Are you sure?"

I smiled. "Eddie would go."

"Yes he would," he told me, and then turned to the crowd. "Brand-new Coco Girl is going to swim big!" As he said this, he made swimming motions with his arms.

Now there was no way I could turn back. Not after that intro. I stripped down to my bathing suit: a bikini top with a pair of board shorts. I gave a little flex, too, to show everybody that the girls were represented.

Mom, Drew, and Kate started chanting, "Darby! Darby! Darby!"

Zach leaned over to me. "Are you crazy?"

I just smiled. "It would appear so."

I looked out into the crowd and locked eyes with Monica. She looked completely pissed, and I couldn't have cared less.

A few more guys joined in, but I was the only girl. Everyone followed us down to the waterline. The moment my foot touched the water, I wanted to turn back and run for cover. It was unbelievably cold.

Most of us stood at the edge of the water and tried to build up the courage. The first to go all the way in was Hawaiian

Rick, and of course that brought a huge cheer from the crowd. A couple more guys ran out and took the plunge, and then my father did the same.

I got up to my calves and was seriously considering bailing out. Then I heard Kate whistle and my mom and Drew chant my name again. Up ahead of me I saw Zach and a few of the other surfers struggling, and I decided that I was going to show them up.

I took a deep breath and just ran forward and dived into the water. Luckily, no one can hear you scream when you're underwater, because I felt the cold deep into my muscles and bones. It was beyond brutal. But when I got back to the surface, I heard a roar from the crowd, and the brutal was a little more bearable. It was one of the most exciting moments of my life.

"Great," Zach called to me. "Now I *have* to go in!"

"That's right, you little girlie man!" I yelled at him, adding a couple of flexes for punctuation.

He used the same technique I did and dived into a wave.

When I sprinted back to the beach, my mom was waiting with one of the big fluffy towels that had been supplied for the swim. I was shivering, and I'm sure that my lips were blue, but I was loving every second of it.

"You are my hero," Kate said, giving me a high five.

"That would hurt if I had any feeling in my hands," I said, flashing a blue-lipped smile. "I have never been so cold in my life. Why did you let me do that?"

I looked over at where Zach was toweling off. Monica was with him and she gave me the stink eye, but I didn't care. I think Zach gave me a little smile, but it was hard to tell because his lips were pretty blue too.

After I got the feeling back in my arms and legs, Kate and I went up to the staging area for the parade. The float actually looked great. Much to my amazement, the conch looked just like a conch, and the sound system really rocked the music. One of the dads used his big four-wheel-drive truck to pull the float, and we all walked alongside it. (I guess this made me an official member of the Spirit Club.)

As we walked down the parade route,

we tossed Valentine candy to the people on the sides of the road. More than a few people recognized me from the Big Swim and gave me an extra cheer.

"You're a celebrity," Kate said to me as she waved to the crowd.

I laughed at the absurdity of it all. It was fun, but I couldn't help but look to the other side of the float, where Zach was walking with Monica. Her evil sixth sense must have known that I was watching, because she made a point of putting her arm around Zach.

True confession time. Despite all my griping, I found marching in a parade to actually be a lot of fun. Maybe it's the wannabe starlet in me, but it was a rush having the people cheer as I walked by. I know that must be a character flaw, but I guess I'm okay with that.

After the parade, everyone went to the park for a huge picnic. There were hot dogs and hamburgers and a guy running around in red tights like a superhero, calling himself Captain St. Valentine. I think it was the kid who dresses up in the conch shell at all the football games.

Kate went over to hang out with Leandro, and I was just standing by myself for a minute. My eyes quickly found Zach, who was goofing around with Monica. He was flashing that epic smile of his, but he was flashing it at her.

"Do you regret it?"

I turned around and saw that my mom had come up behind me.

"Regret what?" I asked.

"Coming today," she said. "Not going to New York."

I thought about it for a moment. "Not at all," I said. "But it's still really hard."

"I know, baby," she said, and she reached over and pushed the hair out of my eyes. "I know."

With absolutely no warning, I started to cry. Not big sobbing tears, but a steady stream. I looked my mom in the eyes and said, "I love him, Mom."

She nodded her head and used her thumb to wipe the tears away. "I know you do."

I saw Dad and Drew heading our way, and I quickly tried to stop crying.

"What's the matter?" Dad asked.

"Residual effects of the Big Swim,"

Mom said. (She is obviously a much better liar than Dad.)

The four of us just hung out for a while, and it occurred to me that when we were in New York, we almost never got a chance to do that. There was so much going on in our lives; it seemed like we were always on the move. Maybe this, right here, was the reason my dad had wanted the change. Our family had never been closer.

There were some more activities after that, including a three-legged race in which Mom and I took home a very respectable third-place ribbon.

Once the picnic ended, everyone headed home to get ready for Cupid's Ball. Even though the ball was held at the hotel, my dad had arranged for a catering group to come in and work the party. That way we could all have fun.

Of course, I wasn't sure how much fun it would be. Unlike the Big Swim, the parade, and the picnic, Cupid's Ball would make my being alone a little more obvious and a little more sucky. Still, I was determined to make it all the way through the celebration, and I wasn't going to stop.

Despite the name, Cupid's Ball is officially a casual dance. After all, it's the beach. There's no reason to bust out the tuxes and gowns. My mom wore a very attractive black dress with spaghetti straps, while my father and brother each wore guayabera shirts and linen pants. (Guayaberas are from Cuba and look kind of like bowling shirts with big pockets and pleat lines. They're really popular in this part of Florida and look very hip.)

I went with a pink-and-white-striped baby-doll dress with a racer back. It was cute and a little sexy. Not that it mattered, considering I had no one to be sexy for. But it fit the mood and even had a big heart button on the front that I thought was perfect for Valentine's Day.

The band was the same one that had played the New Year's Eve party. (Thankfully, they did not play "YMCA" this time.)

"Did I tell you how hot you look?"

I laughed and turned around to see Kate, who looked stunning in a floor-length with a beach print on it.

"Wow," I told her. "That is a great dress."

"Thanks," she said. "By the way, it appears that 'casual' doesn't translate properly into Spanish."

She nodded over toward Leandro, who was dressed to the nines in a shiny silver suit. He smiled and waved.

"It looks good, though," I said.

"That it does," she said with a sigh. "That it does."

The dance floor started off pretty tame, and I managed to get a couple of dances in—one with my dad and another with Leandro's friend from the basketball team. For me the highlight was when some of the older couples got out onto the floor and danced just like Fred Astaire and Ginger Rogers.

Hawaiian Rick showed up wearing a gorgeous lei; he had his long hair slicked back in a ponytail. He even jammed with the band, playing the ukulele for a couple of songs. (It was what I imagined Iz looked like when he performed.)

Zach and Monica arrived about an hour after the party started. I tried not to obsess about them, but it was hard. I must have spent about fifteen minutes just staring at them as they got some punch and talked to friends.

Finally, the band started playing a slow song, and they went out onto the dance floor. That was more than I could handle. I wasn't going to sit there and watch the girl I hated dance with the boy I loved in the same building that I lived in.

It was just too much.

I slipped out the back so I wouldn't have to walk past my parents and took the stairs up to the third floor. I went into my room and climbed over the balcony. (This, by the way, is not so easy to do in a dress.)

I grabbed my folding chair and found a spot with a great view of the ocean. In some ways it was just like New Year's Eve. I was on the roof and could hear the party going on two floors below me.

But unlike New Year's, this time I didn't look out at the beach and hate it. In the past six weeks, I had come to love it. It was fun and it was pretty and it was home.

The moon was full and lit up the ocean. I just sat there and looked out at the water and started to cry. I don't even know how long I did. It just all came out. And it wasn't just because of Zach. It was for all different reasons—good and bad. I just cried until my eyes felt like they had completely cried themselves dry.

I cried so much that I didn't even hear him coming up behind me.

"Are you finished?"

It was Zach.

"I didn't want to interrupt you," he said. "And I don't have a handkerchief. But if you'd like, you could use my sleeve."

"No, thanks," I snorted, halfway between a laugh and a sob. "I brought my own."

I held up a wad of Kleenex.

"You come prepared. I like that about you."

"What are you doing up here?" I asked him.

He smiled. "I was looking for you, actually. I looked all around downstairs and out on the beach. And then I remembered that you were out here on New Year's Eve, and I thought I might be able to find you here."

"Well, you found me," I said, as I tried to wipe the gunk out of my eyes and nose.

"I also found this," he said, pulling my letter out of his pocket. He flapped it back and forth a couple of times. "It is some letter . . . and I can't get it out of my mind. Which makes sense when you consider that I can't get you out of my mind either."

"Wow," I said. "That's . . . interesting."

"You know what else I found," he said as he walked closer to me. "I found out that Monica Baylor isn't really that nice a person."

"No comment," I said, opting out of venting about Monica.

He went on. "And I also found that on Valentine's you really want to be with the right girl."

I stood up, and we were face to face.

"I don't drive a Porsche; I drive a beat-up old Jeep. The most expensive shoes I own are a thirty-dollar pair of Converse. And the closest my father has ever gotten to Donald Trump was watching an episode of *The Apprentice*."

"None of those things impress me," I said.

"What does?"

"You do," I said as I lost myself in his eyes. "You impress me so very much."

I thought he was going to kiss me, but he didn't.

"I also found a shark's tooth with the letter. Did you find it on the beach?"

"Without any help." I nodded. "My very first one."

"If it's your first one, I think you should keep it."

He reached into his pocket and pulled out the shark's tooth. Only it was now attached to a necklace.

"Where did you get that?"

"I've had it forever," he said. "But the tooth fell out a long time ago. It turns out the one you found is a perfect fit."

He put the necklace around my neck and attached the clasp in back.

"Listen," he whispered.

"To what?"

"The band."

From down below in the ballroom we could hear the band playing. In keeping with the theme of the day, they were doing their version of "Sea of Love." It was a song that we had heard over and over, only now, as Zach whispered the lyrics to me, they had an entirely new meaning.

*Do you remember when we met?*
*That was the day I knew you were my pet.*
*I want to tell you how much I love you.*

We danced to the music on the rooftop. And the slow dance turned into a very long and slow kiss. Suffice it to say that much toe-curling ensued.

# Epilogue

"Did I tell you how hot you look?" Kate asked.

It was spring break, and we were about to go out dancing with Zach and Leandro.

"I think you may have mentioned it," I said. "But thanks for the confidence boost."

To her great surprise Kate seemed to have found a good match with her Argentinean point guard. She even enrolled in an intensive Spanish-language program at the community college. (I also turned her onto *El gigante ocho setenta* out of Miami *"Todas las clásicas, todo el tiempo."* After all, it had been good for me and Zach.)

So far Zach has tried to teach me how to surf and tried to teach me how to drive. I've struggled with both, but I stayed up on my board once for more than thirty seconds and have three times managed to get the Jeep all the way into fourth gear without stalling out.

I, by the way, am not the only new surfer in the family. Mom is Hawaiian Rick's star pupil. Ever the competitor, she's got her eye on a senior women's competition in June.

It turned out to be a stroke of good fortune that I did not go with Brendan to Hadley Montgomery's Valentine's bash. At the party Brendan met Had's cousin Heather, who in addition to playing clarinet and field hockey is really impressed by expensive shoes and Donald Trump stories.

Brendan is officially out of my life and officially off of my screen saver. The pictures of New York have all been replaced by shots of Coconut Beach and my ever-growing list of Florida friends. There is an especially high concentration of pictures of Zach surfing. (Can I help it that he's photogenic when he's shirtless?)

Speaking of shirtless, my father has begun taking occasional jogs with my mother in preparation for next year's Big Swim. He still sneaks a fair amount of Cap'n Crunch, but he's making progress.

Once a month my family and Zach's family go together to Rico's Fish Camp for the Friday fish fry. It's fast becoming a tradition. (Coconut Beach seems overrun with traditions.) Not only is my mom okay with us eating all the fried foods, but she even helps lead the Cookie Monster cheer.

All my college mail has finally come in. I've been wait-listed by Vassar and accepted at Sarah Lawrence, NYU, and the University of Florida. Even though I only applied to Florida as a favor to my father, Zach convinced me to visit the campus with him during our break. (He was also accepted there, so that may have something to do with my change of heart.) We drove up in the Jeep and listened to Iz the whole way.

"There's a few problems with the school you should know about," he warned me as we tooled along the highway.

"What are they?" I asked as my finger

twirled around the shark's tooth necklace I was wearing.

"First of all," he said. "It's not in New York. In fact it's not even in a big city. It's just stuck there in the middle of god-forsaken Florida. It's everything you said you weren't looking for."

I smiled and thought about the best advice my mother has ever given me.

"So what?"

## About the Author

Jamie Ponti grew up in Atlantic Beach, Florida, a town very similar to the fictional setting of this book. A writer and television producer, Jamie has also written the young-adult novels *Animal Attraction* and *Prama*. If you want to find out more about Jamie, visit www.JamiePonti.com.

I spit a jaw-achingly huge gob of bubble gum into my palm and look at my watch. Three . . . two . . . one. The shrill ring pierces throughout Snowcrest High School, sending the last few students scurrying to their first-period classes.

The hall is as vacant as the library-sponsored Don't Forget to Read During the Summer popcorn-and-punch party last May. By that I mean no one's out here except for Mrs. Leonard (the librarian) and *moi*.

Um, yeah. I was there. But only 'cause I was trying to fix up our school's And Literacy For All chapter prez with her crush. Neither of whom showed up. Which explains why Mrs. Leonard thinks I'm some sort of superdevout bookworm who just loves volunteering in the periodicals section. I can already tell that my locker placement—right next to the library—is going to prove problematic. Hoping she doesn't notice me (and heaven forbid venture over for a chitchat) I pretend to be searching for something in my locker. Only it's the first day of school, so besides a tiny magnetic mirror, a tube of Kiss & Tell lip gloss, and my reserve of loose-leaf paper, the locker's empty.

Mrs. Leonard's trademark blue suede pumps *clack-clack* back into her bookly haven, and I relax. By now my gum has started to harden, so I pop it back in my mouth, give it a good thorough chew, and divide it in half with my tongue and teeth.

One more glance to ensure the coast is clear, and I stick the gum wads in the doorjamb of my locker, one up top and one below. Then I shut the door, squeezing it firmly closed.

After a few seconds I do the combo and try to open my locker. It won't budge. I try again, wiggling it more forcefully. No luck.

Here's the plan: Anna Black (my client's crush) will be trying to get her locker unstuck (after I've performed Operation Gum Stick to it), and right when she's starting to freak out about getting her first-ever tardy mark, Hunter Davidson (my client) will show up like a knight in shining armor to successfully open it. Naturally, she'll bat her eyelashes, swoon, and sigh a heartfelt "My hero." And they'll live happily ever after.

Okay, maybe it won't happen *exactly* like that, but it will definitely put Hunter on her radar and make a terrific first impression. That's a big step in the whole process. *Huge*, actually. And yes, maybe this whole scenario sounds a bit old-fashioned, but I've had my matchmaking business for six months now, and if you ask any of my male clients, bringing chivalry back definitely has its rewards.

I kick my locker. Still won't open. Hmmm.

"Need a hand?" It's a soft Southern drawl, and when I whirl around, I'm half expecting to see Matthew McConaughey. Had it really been Matthew, I don't think

I'd be any less spellbound. The guy standing before me—tall, longish sandy-colored hair, dark blue eyes with long lashes, sexy smile, a dimple in his left cheek . . . *erm*. What did he say? Oh yeah.

"Sure. Thanks." I scratch my head while he wrestles with the locker. "I have no clue why the darn thing keeps sticking on me. Guess I'll have to find the janitor."

"Naw," he says, examining the doorjamb. "I'm fixin' to get it." He takes his leather wallet out of his back pocket, unfolds it, and extracts a toothpick. Then he proceeds to poke at the top of the locker door, where I stuck one wad of gum. The gum loosens, and he continues jiggling and joggling the door until it flies open.

"Did you put that there?" he asks, pointing at the gum that's still stuck to the bottom part of the jamb. (I don't even want to think about where the other piece ended up.)

Oh, the humility. I just love admitting I'm crazy to hot new guys. "Well, it was kind of an experiment," I say, fully realizing how lame that sounds. "For a class," I add, in case he thinks I am doing the proverbial damsel-in-distress thing to meet a guy. Sure, I stage these types of things all the time so my clients can get with their crushes, but I wouldn't use such tactics myself.

And it turns out I won't be using this particular tactic to help Hunter, either. Mark Operation Gum Stick a failure.

Maybe if I stuff some paper in the jamb . . . ?

"Well, thanks for the help," I say, realizing that The Hot New Guy is just standing there, staring at me. What, do I have something in my nose? Or lipstick on my tooth? I'm not really used to wearing lipstick, but my sister, Maddie, just got a new shade and insisted I try it out when she drove me to school this morning.

"No problem." He turns to leave, and I take this opportunity to check myself in the locker mirror. Hmm. Nose and tooth check clear.

"Hey! You're new around here, right?" I know I'm stating the obvious, but at least it might postpone his vanishing act. And boy, I could definitely use a little more of this eye candy. Besides, I'm already late, and there's no difference between a little late and a lot late on one's attendance record.

"Just moved here from Texas," he says, walking backward so he can face me.

"Cool." I twirl my hair around my finger. Does it look as cute when I do this as when Maddie does it? Probably not, since her gorgeous auburn mane doesn't know the meaning of Bad Hair Day, while my just-long-enough-for-a-ponytail brown hair—*not* chestnut or nutmeg or pecan or hazelnut or walnut or espresso or chocolate or any of those deluxe (and suspiciously yummy-sounding) colors—could very well be the founder and president. Of Bad Hair Day, that is.

"I guess so," The Hot New Guy says. "Well, I'll see ya around. Gotta get to class. And next time you need a place to put your gum, try a trash can."

"Right. Of course. No problem. See you. Bye." Please tell me that dreadful giggling isn't spewing out of my mouth.

He swaggers (he actually *swaggers*!) down the hall and disappears into the east wing. Which is just as well, because I should probably be getting to class myself.

I gather my chemistry book and folder and scurry down the hall to room 116. Mr. Foley is writing something on the blackboard, and for a split second I frolic in the belief that I'm getting off scot-free. But as I slip into an empty seat in the back, he twirls around and pegs me with an *I caught you* glare. I swallow and then smile, hoping I'm the essence of innocence. Mr. Foley glances down at a piece of paper on his desk—the class roster, I presume?—and says, "And you are . . . ?"

This is my second semester with Mr. Foley (he also teaches driver's ed), so you'd think he'd know who I am by now. But I guess I'm not surprised. I'm pretty good at blending in. Maybe that's why I'm so good at my job. A flamboyant, center-stage type would have a hard time keeping her identity under wraps, I'd think.

"Sasha Finnegan." I don't have a perfect record like Anna Black does at her school, but still, it's a little embarrassing to be put on the spot like this. And the instant I catch a glimpse of a familiar sandy-haired, blue-eyed, Texas-A&M-T-shirted guy in the second row, my embarrassment modifier jumps to *totally*.

Mr. Foley makes a gross guttural noise and says, "If it's okay with you, Sasha, I'd like to start class *on time* from now on."

"Yes, sir," I say, squirming in my seat.

Mr. Foley launches into a lecture, but it's impossible to concentrate on all those formulas and definitions. Didn't he get the memo that today is all about fun and games? Who ever heard of a teacher who makes his students actually *work* on the first day of school? While he yammers on, I keep looking out the window. Not that there's anything interesting happening in the juniper bush out there, but if I tilt my head just so, I have an excellent peripheral view of The Hot New Guy.

My faith in the minute hand is restored when the bell rings and we all gather our folders and backpacks. "Go directly to the gym for the back-to-school assembly," Mr. Foley calls over the din.

I look for The Hot New Guy in the hall. (I'll just call him THNG until I figure out his name.) But, apparently, the swarm of high schoolers has swallowed him whole. Any other day I'd skip the gaudy spectacle of school spirit otherwise known as the pep rally, but Maddie's been working really hard on her routine, and what kind of sister would I be to miss her debut as varsity cheerleader? And since THNG is new and naive and everything, he'll probably be at the pep rally. Not that I'm stalking him.

Squinting, I leave the fluorescent-lit hallway and enter the sunshiny brightness of the gymnasium. The freshly buffed wooden court gleams, and a collage of hand-painted banners scream *Snowcrest Rams Rule!* and *SHS is #1!* from the walls. The enormous room is buzzing with first-day-of-school exuberance.

"Sasha! Over here!"

Twisting around, I spot Yasmin waving frantically from the tip-top of the bleachers. As usual she's dressed to thrill, her first-day-of-school ensemble consisting of pin-striped trouser shorts and a red satin wraparound top à la Hilary Duff at the Teen Choice Awards.

I muscle my way up the steps and

"excuse me, pardon me, *ouch*!" my way to her side. "Why do you always have to sit in the nosebleed section?" I ask, slightly out of breath. How she climbed all those stairs in three-inch heels, I'll never know.

"'Cause I get to scam all the hot guys," she answers, not even caring that the boys sitting around us are all listening in. She tucks her shiny black hair behind a thoroughly adorned ear and says, "Oh my God, Sasha. You look darling. Where'd you get that skirt?"

I have to look to remember what I'm wearing. Right. It's Tommy Hilfiger, and it flares out a little on the bottom. The flare part makes my thighs look a little less . . . well, a little *less*. "Maddie's closet," I say. "But it falls off of her, so she bequeathed it to me." Sure, I can fit into a few of Maddie's sweatshirts and shoes, but it's not every day I can say I'm wearing something of hers. I should be psyched about scoring a brand-new, this-season skirt, but what I wouldn't give to be the Skinny Sister for once.

Yas nods understandingly. "Yeah, that super-stretchy denim can be totally misleading. She should've bought one two sizes smaller than what she normally wears." Then she faces forward and says, "Oh, look. It's starting!"

First, the student body is treated to the procession of teachers and teachers' aides, who march solemnly across the court and file into the front few rows. Next, this year's starched-and-pressed student council parades in, treating their subjects to a sequence of waves, thumbs-up, fist pumps, and one particularly jarring fingers-in-mouth whistle. I feel a headache coming on. And when the marching band makes its big entrance, banging and clanging out something that sounds roughly like the Snowcrest High School fight song, I wonder: Can a headache spread to one's whole body?

Yasmin elbows me and gestures (not very subtly) at a potential hottie. He's sitting on the ground level, so it's not like I could see what he looks like even if he were facing us. But the back of his head looks pretty cute, so I smile and nod, wishing there were a volume control on the band. Yasmin bites her lower lip as that *I'm gonna get him* gleam settles in her exotic eyes.

The JV cheerleaders take center stage in their new black-and-red uniforms, doing round-offs and aerials and complicated twisty-tricks as they shout, "Goooooo, Snowcrest!" Then they reach out their arms and give the spirit-fingers salute to the varsity squad, who's hot on their trail. Launching into their routine, which is thankfully accompanied by a CD and not the marching band, the varsity cheerleaders fling their tiny bodies around in perfect time.

They're . . . *good*. Great, even. I can't take my eyes off of them.

And Maddie looks the best of all. She's zipping through her back handsprings like she has actual springs growing out of her feet. Oh my God, did she just do a whip back? And now she's being launched to the tip-top of a pyramid. All those cheerleader camps have really paid off!

"Maddie looks amazing," Yas says, pointing at my sis as if I need help locating her. Just look around. *Everybody* is checking her out.

Then I notice him. THNG. He's sitting

four rows in front of me, two o'clock. I can see from here that he's zeroed in on Maddie. Is that a trickle of drool on his chin? Well, I shouldn't be surprised. I mean, Maddie is drop-dead gorgeous—all silky auburn hair, green eyes, and freakishly long legs. If she weren't my sister, I'd definitely hate her.

Maddie does a dead man, falling backward into three other cheerleaders' hands. Then they pitch her up and she does another dead man, forward. The student body goes wild as she pops up and flings her hair back into place. She joins the others in their little "Go! Fight! Win!" cheer. It looks like Maddie Finnegan has given Snowcrest High a terrible case of school spirit. I just hope the whole place doesn't have to be quarantined.

As soon as Yasmin drops me off at my house, I grab a snack and run up to my room. I shuck my sweater and sprawl out on my bed. I get out my laptop and write a quick update e-mail to Hunter, letting him know a brilliant plan is in the works and to hang tight for further direction. After I hit send, I notice there's a message in my inbox waiting to be opened.

Subj: Request 4 Help
Date: Sept. 9, 2:47 PM Mountain Standard Time
From: 66Chevy@kmail.com
To: MissMatch@MissMatch4Hire.com

Dear Miss Match,
My friend Caden Baxter told me about you.
You really came thru for him and I'm hoping you
can work the same magic for me?
Here's the deal. There's a girl at my school. Not just
any girl—she's a goddess. I want to ask her to the
homecoming dance, but I doubt she even knows
I exist. Anyway, homecoming is only a month away,
so I know I'm asking a lot. I'll pay you extra.
Let me know.
Thanks,
Derek Urban

Derek's e-mail isn't anything out of the ordinary. I get e-mails like this every week. It's all part of the job. But when I start reading the Miss Match Questionnaire he so kindly filled out in full, I about fall off my bed. I blink three times and reread the first line:

NAME OF CRUSH: Maddie Finnegan

This Derek guy wants me to fix him up with *my sister*!

I've worked wonders with beauties and beasts, princes and paupers, city mice and country mice, angels and devils . . . but never anything so close to home. Literally.

Sure, since I work locally (it's not like I can jet set all over the world) there's always the chance I'll know or recognize a client or the person he or she is all into. But I never thought I'd see the day that a guy would pay me to fix him up with my own flesh-and-blood sister.

Who is this Derek guy, anyway? Am I going to like him enough to help him get a date with my sister? And who's to say Maddie will even give him the time of day? Does he realize that she's dated the dreamiest guys from Provo to Logan, and one who just left for his sophomore year at Yale? Or that Maddie changes boyfriends as often as she changes her Abercrombie & Fitch jeans?

Then again, he *did* offer to pay me extra, and after six long months I'm only one gig away from clearing my debt to Mrs. Woosely once and for all. Besides, when have I ever backed down from a challenge? I guess I can always refund his money and refuse to make the match if I don't feel right about it . . . right? So really, what's to lose?

I'll just have to get to know this Derek Urban before I fix him up with Maddie.

I hit reply and type:

Subj: Important Message from M.M.
Date: Sept. 9, 10:03 PM Mountain Standard Time
From: MissMatch@MissMatch4Hire.com
To: 66Chevy@kmail.com

Dear Derek,
Greetings, and congratulations on finding Miss Match. You're about to embark on a romantic adventure, and I'm here to provide the magic to get it all started.
Meet me at Subway at noon on Friday. Since homecoming's just around the corner, every minute counts. I'll be wearing a red T-shirt with a white heart.
Ciao for now,
M.M.

⭐

It's Friday, 11:54 a.m. I'm sitting in the far corner of the hard yellow booth at the Subway across the street from Snowcrest. It smells like yeast and onions in here. The September sun blares through the window and penetrates my scalp. High schoolers roll in and out, but no one pays any attention to me.

My cell phone rings. It's Yasmin. "Where are you?" she asks.

Ugh. I'm such a bad friend. "I'm sorry, girl. I totally spaced eating with you. I'm actually having a working lunch today."

Ever since the day she suggested I turn my matchmaking hobby into an actual moneymaking profession, Yasmin has been my loyal and fabulous sidekick. Not only is she the reigning yearbook editor, she has a flair for digging up everything and anything that's scandalicious. She's an expert secret- and gossip-miner. Seriously. I'm floored with all the "news" she's privy to. Plus, while I tend to blend in, she's a hottie with a look-at-me attitude, and that proves useful from time to time. Miss Match wouldn't be such a success if it weren't for Yas.

"Sure, just stand me up. What, am I supposed to eat alone?" she says with a slight whine in her voice. "Might as well banish me to Loserdom."

"Maybe you can go with Hilary and Sami?" I suggest. "They're probably at Arctic Circle."

"Okay. Oh, wait. Brian's waving at me. Maybe he'll split his PB&J with me."

"Sounds yummy."

"Yeah, I love peanut butter."

"No, I mean Brian." I've always thought Yas and Brian would make the perfect couple, and I'm even more sure of it now. Long gone are the lanky limbs and pimples of yesteryear. The summer's been good to him, and Yas noticed too. "Did you know Brian's the hottie you were checking out at the pep rally?" I ask.

After a pause, she says, "Really? That's weird."

"There's no denying he's looking *good* these days, Yas."

"Yeah, I guess you're right." Her voice sounds a bit distant, like she's holding her phone away from her mouth. "Well, I'd better let you go, so you can work."

We hang up just as someone slides up to the booth, hovering over me. Oh my God, it's THNG. "Hi!" he says, putting his hands on the table and leaning forward.

I'm sure I've got some major red-face issues just about now. Man, he's cute. He's wearing baggy, olive-colored shorts and flip-flops. I can't help but notice what nice legs he has: long and muscular with a left-over summer tan. He leans down and whispers in my ear, "So, what's up, Miss Match?" *Oooooh*, that accent!

Hang on.

Did he just call me . . . ? No way. THNG is Derek Urban? THNG wants me to fix him up with my sister?

My jaw falls to the floor.

# Funny. Fresh. Fabulous.

Don't miss these books by Julie Linker:

From Simon Pulse

Published by Simon & Schuster

# Get smitten with these scrumptious British treats:

### Prada Princesses
by Jasmine Oliver

Three friends tackle
the high-stakes world
of fashion school.

### 10 Ways to Cope
with Boys
by Caroline Plaisted

What every girl *really*
needs to know.

### Does Snogging
Count as Exercise?
by Helen Salter

For any girl who's
tongue-tied around boys.

**From Simon Pulse · Published by Simon & Schuster**

The adorable, delicious—
and très stylish—adventures of
Imogene are delighting readers
around the globe.
Don't miss these darling
new favorites!

*A Girl Like Moi*

*Project Paris*

*Accidentally Fabulous*

by Lisa Barham

From Simon Pulse
Published by Simon & Schuster

# Need a distraction?

Amy Belasen & Jacob Osborn

Anita Liberty

Julie Linker

Teri Brown